LAWRENCE

THE BROTHERS OF HASTINGS RANCH SERIES
BOOK FOUR

By Katharine E. Hamilton

ISBN-13: 978-1-7358125-4-0

Lawrence

www.katharinehamilton.com

Cover Design by Kerry Prater.

To Brad.
Because I just love you more and more every day,
and that's super cool.

Acknowledgments

Thanks to my cover designer, Kerry Prater, for yet another awesome cover and for dealing with my pickiness.

Thank you to my editor, Lauren Hanson. A new baby hasn't slowed her down, and I'm forever grateful.

My husband, Brad. He gives me so much insight into the ranching world, it's crazy. I don't capture near enough of it, but I do my best.

To my two little men, Everett and West. I love being your Momma.

And to my readers. Thanks for coming along on another series with me.

H

Chapter One

"*I've got two steaks.* One medium rare," She placed the platter in front of a hungry Philip Hastings. "and one rare." The other plate settled in front of a ravenous Clint, Philip's younger brother. "You two guys enjoy." Ruby Cole bustled away from the table and back towards the counter, already swiping more plates from the cook's window to deliver to another table. Her sneakers squeaked on the freshly mopped floor as she passed the table that hosted the accident-prone toddler who'd already knocked his parents' drinks over. Twice. She didn't mind, though. She loved that people felt comfortable bringing their little ones into the diner. And she also loved to see them enjoy time together over her food. She placed the dishes in front of the two older men passing through Parks, Texas on a business trip. "Here you go, gentlemen. Anything else I can get you?"

"Hey, Slop!" A voice called from across the diner and Ruby cringed at the horrible nickname she'd been tagged with since she was a child. No matter how hard she tried and changed, people still saw her as the skinned knees and rough and tumble-haired little girl in a stained dress.

"Excuse me." She nodded a farewell to the gentlemen and hurried over towards Clint Hastings. "Really? You have to yell across the restaurant?"

"We need you to settle a debate."

Ruby rolled her eyes. "What is it this time?"

"Philip here doesn't seem to think I should ask Helena's dad and brother out to the ranch to look it over before I talk with Graham. I say, bring them on the ranch, show them the place, and then present their feedback to Graham. You know, from a prospective hunter's point of view."

"If you bring strangers onto that ranch without first consulting Graham, I will stand by with a shovel at the ready, because you will be digging your own grave, Clint."

Philip laughed and nodded in agreement as Clint leaned back in his chair in frustration. "Well, we all know he will say no."

"So you're trying to think of ways to undermine him? Not cool."

"That's what I said. Plus, Helena isn't too keen on that plan either," Philip added, sharing his new girlfriend's feelings on the matter.

Ruby rested a hand on Clint's shoulder. "Be patient. Present facts, numbers, thorough plans in a calm and professional manner and then maybe Graham will listen. But if you go in there with an attitude—"

"I don't have an att—"

Ruby narrowed her gaze on the brother, and he let her continue. "Keep calm and collected. Even if you get frustrated. If you get all riled up, then Graham will get all riled up and nothing will come of it."

Clint took an oversized bite of his steak and closed his eyes as he savored. Talking around the meat in his mouth, he looked to Ruby. "I think this steak makes me feel better."

She grinned. "That's what I'm here for." Giving him one more encouraging pat, she turned to walk back to the counter when Jimmy, the new vet technician for her friend Alice Wilkenson, walked into the diner. He waved, his eyes immediately seeking her out. A flutter tickled her stomach when he walked to the bar and sat, waiting for her to come and talk with him. He'd been coming around more often now that he lived behind the diner in Alice's old house. Alice had moved into the guesthouse at the Hastings brothers' ranch along with her friend Julia McComas. Both women dated one of the brothers, though Julia and Graham had recently gotten engaged. Alice and Calvin, the second oldest Hastings brother, had decided to take their friendship one step further, and everyone knew it would be a match made in heaven. Ruby glanced towards Clint and Philip, Philip being the last of the Hastings brothers to take a tumble into the love department when the new agricultural pharmaceutical representative, Helena Shaw, had swooped in a few months ago to shake up his world. It was sweet, Ruby thought, to see her childhood friends fall for beautiful, strong, and kind women.

She'd grown up with the brothers. For as long as she remembered, she was always trailing alongside at least one of them. In elementary school, she and Hayes Hastings were in the same class, though Lawrence, a year older than the two of them, joined them in a plethora of shenanigans. Her parents had left her, at the age of two, with her grandparents. Not cut out for parenting, they quickly changed their minds on keeping their only daughter and headed God only knew where. At the age of sixteen, Ruby lost her grandfather. At the age of seventeen, her grandmother followed him into glory. And though they did not give her a fancy life, they gave her a good life. And even after their deaths, they made sure she'd be taken care of by deeding her the diner and their house. She'd attempted hiring a manager for the diner so she could go to masseuse school, but it was short-lived. Sloppy's Diner fell into a deep pit that took a few years for Ruby to claw out of. But she had, with the help of the Hastings family and Annie and Henry, the loving older couple who took it upon themselves to love on any wayward child. Now her family was loud, stubborn, numerous, and wonderful. The Hastings brothers took her welfare as their personal responsibility, and on every single day of the week, one of them stopped by the diner or reached out to her to see how she was doing.

"Jimmy, how was work today?" She swiped a towel over the bar top as she waited for the cute vet tech to let her know what he'd like for his supper.

"Ruby." He grinned. He had a nice face, though Seth, the youngest Hastings brother, had commented on Jimmy's long nose more than a time or two. Ruby didn't mind it. It fit his face, and he wore his hair shaggy and around the collar instead of clean, cut, and cropped. "I think I will keep it light tonight."

"I have some soup if that sounds okay?"

"If you and Sal made it, then I'm sure it's the best," Jimmy complimented the oversized cook in the back while Ruby hurried to the kitchen to fetch him a bowl.

"Good to see you, Jimmy." Clint walked up to the bar and shook the man's hand. "Long day?"
"You could say that." Jimmy perked up when Ruby returned, her brow slightly rising in surprise as Clint sat next to him.

"Did you need something Clint?" She looked towards his table and noticed Philip had left.

"Was going to sweet talk some soup off of you for Lawrence."

"He still out working?"

"No. Actually he didn't work at all today. Sick as a dog."

Sympathy laced Ruby's words. "Oh no, I hope he's okay."

"He's fine. Just a bit of a sinus infection, I think. That rain that blew in a few weeks ago gave everything a little bloom and he's just got a sensitive nose, apparently."

"Let me go get him some." Ruby darted back into the kitchen.

"So, you sweet on her?" Clint asked Jimmy, nodding in Ruby's direction.

Jimmy shrugged. "I like her. She's a friendly face. Doesn't hurt that it's a pretty one."

"Slop's like family to us. She's one of the good ones here in Parks."

"Is this you giving me the warning talk?" Jimmy asked.

"No. Just saw her disappointment at me sitting beside you when she came out of the back. Seems she likes having you around. I was just seeing if that feeling was mutual."

"It is," Jimmy answered, and then grew quiet as Ruby returned with not only a container of soup, but slices of fresh bread and crackers.

"Tell Law I hope he gets to feeling better."

"I will." Clint fished money out of his wallet and laid it on the bar. "For Phil's supper too." He told her when her eyes widened at the amount he dropped on the counter. The brothers were always good about overpaying for their meals. Again, she knew it was one of their subtle ways of making sure she was taken care of. Thanking Clint, she stuffed a few napkins into the sack before he walked away.

"I hate that Lawrence is sick," Ruby commented. "He rarely goes under. But when he does..." She shook her head on a low whistle.

"What? He gets really sick?" Jimmy asked.

"No." Ruby stifled a small chuckle. "He becomes the biggest pain. A big baby."

"Ah. Well, I'm not so wonderful myself when I don't feel well."

"He and Graham just turn into flat out sour pusses at the first sign of a sniffle," Ruby continued. "Then they become snarly bears."

"Well, maybe your soup will help him."

"It will. I added extra broth to his."

"Secretly taking care of him?"

"It's what we do around here." She held up Clint's wad of cash.

Jimmy polished off the last of his soup, nudging the bowl aside, and taking one last long sip of his sweet tea. "Well, I best be headed to the house. I need to feed Roly. Thanks for supper again."

"No problem." Ruby smiled, liking that Jimmy was tenderhearted and had a pet he cared about. She'd recently become a pet owner when Calvin had found a box of puppies on the side of the road. Though her dog spent most of its time on the porch of the diner with the town staple, Roughneck Randy, she liked having it around. Especially at night. For whatever reason, Parks had been a stopping point for oil roughnecks and work crews the last few weeks. The men were rowdy, rude, and rambunctious. And she liked the added security of canine company on her walk up the street towards home. None had bothered her, other than a bit of catcalling, but in the diner... well, she'd swatted away a few stray hands here and there over the last couple of weeks. *Nothing she couldn't handle*, she reminded herself. She was used to handling the diner by herself. She'd been running it for years. But when her safety grew questionable, she always became overly cautious to make sure her walks home were quick. She could always call Philip to come to the diner if she needed an escort home, but she didn't like involving the Hastings brothers any more than she had to because all of them were protective of her. And should they come across a man disrespecting her, she couldn't say whether or not the Hastings would just flat out kill the man. So for society's sake, she toughed it up and walked home alone.

She glanced at her watch as Jimmy walked out the front door, followed by the remaining patrons. She'd never had to enforce her open hours. People seemed to respect the fact she wanted to get home at a decent time and drifted out before closing time. She followed the last of the customers to the door and flipped the sign.

She peeked outside. "Hungry?" she asked Roughneck Randy.

"No ma'am. I'm still full from that wonderful lunch you gave me. But I think Fido is pretty hungry."

"His name is Porter," Ruby corrected, leaning down and fluffing the puppy behind his ears. "Come on boy." She opened the door for the puppy to walk inside. He obediently laid on the rug by the doors as she locked them behind her.

Sal glanced out of the open cook window. "All done?"

"Yep."

"You're probably over the worst of it by now, then. You take something?"

"Allergy medicine and some fru-fru tea Julia gave me, which I hate to admit, wasn't that bad."

"Does anything bad come from Julia?" Clint asked, smiling at the thought of his brother Graham's fiancé.

"No. Probably not," Lawrence agreed. "Thanks for bringing me some soup from Sloppy's."

"Don't mention it."

A loud slap had Lawrence wrenching forward as his brother Hayes walked up, slapping his leather gloves against his thigh after swatting him. "Lookin' perkier, Law." He grinned.
"Shut up."

"Oh... not there yet, huh?" Hayes chuckled. "Was going to see if you would help me out after lunch with the tack room."

"Depends on what we get done at the pens."

"Well, I'll be out there 'til late. I want to get it done today," Hayes continued.

"And the last thing I want to do right now is get covered in more dust and hay. So if you want my help, you'll have to wait." Lawrence's poor mood was uncharacteristic, but not when he was sick.

Hayes laughed. "Ah. Right. Yeah. I forget you turn sour when you don't feel well. Yeah, best you not help me, then. I'm determined to have a good day, and I don't want you ruining it."

"I'm not sour." Lawrence barked and then shook his head as his brothers laughed at his expense. He stopped in his tracks again and sneezed another round. "Ugh!" Frustrated, he looked up at the sky and prayed for patience and healing.

"Alright, that does it." Graham's voice drifted towards them as he walked to catch up. "Take another day, Lawrence."

"I'm fine."

"No, you're not. You can barely see. You can barely move without sneezing, and I for one would hate to wear a welding mask if it were me."

Lawrence groaned. "Right. Well, I can do something else. I can help Cal with the clearing."

"Nope. I want you to get well." Graham gave an encouraging slap on his back.

H

Chapter Two

"What about this one?"

Helena asked, holding up a crisp blue sundress.

"She already has a blue dress," Alice called out from across the clothing racks.

"And so do we all," Helena added. "There's always room for one more."

"I was thinking navy." Julia held up a slim-fitting cocktail dress. Helena nodded while Alice pulled a face. "Well, I know you're not going to like it because it's not a plaid button up shirt." Julia laughed as she carried it over to the fitting room

Ruby stood in and draped it over the door. "Here's another one," she stated.

Ruby handed over her discards and Julia began hanging the various dresses back on their hangers.

"So I'm not one to dress shop." Alice shrugged. "But I appreciate a nice dress. That one you let me borrow a couple of weeks ago had Calvin drooling all night." She grinned. "He sort of just stared at me like this all evening." She hung her mouth open and the other two women laughed.

"The power of a killer dress." Helena held up a pink one and Julia and Alice both shook their heads. "Philip is used to seeing me in dresses. I think I made him swoon when he saw me in jeans and boots."

"It's good to throw one on them every now and then." Julia handed the rejected garments to an employee and walked back towards the clothing racks.

"Alright, I think I like this one." Ruby stepped out in the navy dress Julia had selected.

"Winner, winner, chicken dinner." Helena smiled as Alice nodded in agreement.

"You look stunning, Ruby," Julia complimented.

"Jimmy won't know what to do." Alice grinned as Ruby hurried back into the dressing room before she grew too embarrassed. It felt nice shopping with the girls. She'd never quite had such friendships and she was thankful. Annie typically came along, but she was weeding her flower beds today and deemed Julia, Helena, and Alice as plenty of help. She studied her reflection a moment, the dress simple but classic. Though her hair was short, she had bangs that swooped to the side and would be nicely styled to the left. She tapped her lips, normally painted a bold color and debated what shade she wanted to rock later. Red. Definitely red. Smiling, she quickly changed back into her jeans and top to meet up with the other women.

"Look, all I'm saying is that we should all go out together," Alice mentioned as Ruby joined in on the conversation. "What say you, Slop? Quadruple date?"

"Tonight?"

"No, like sometime next week or so."

"Well, if things go well tonight, then sure. I should probably see if Jimmy is really into me before I commit." Ruby flushed at the possibility.

"He'd be a fool not to be." Julia waited to the side as Ruby handed her cash to the employee and paid for her dress.

"So that's settled then. Next Thursday," Alice confirmed, looking to Helena for her confirmation as well. "We'll eat at Graham's place since he has the biggest table."

"You think we can pull off a meal without some of the other brothers stopping by for some food?" Julia laughed, knowing that since she'd arrived at the ranch, she'd found herself not only cooking for Graham each night, which she loved, but for at least one brother as well. They seemed to rotate their evenings.

"I'll warn 'em off." Alice glanced down at her phone that vibrated softly in her hand. "Sorry, I've got to take this. It's my dad at the clinic." She hurried out of the shop to wait on the sidewalk, her hands moving as she chatted with her dad about one of their animal patients.

Ruby, Julia, and Helena stepped out of the store and waited for Alice to finish up her conversation before walking towards an outdoor patio. When the doc stuffed her phone into her pocket, she fell into step beside them.

"So, Sloppy," Alice began. "what is it about Jimmy that has you interested?"

Ruby smiled. "He's nice."

"That's it?" Alice asked.

Laughing, Helena nudged Alice. "Let her finish."

"Yes, he is nice," Ruby reiterated. "And cute in a sort of a boyish charm way. And fun. He comes by the diner every evening and ends my day on a good note."

"Which is important," Julia added.

"You have any tidbits to add, Alice? Since you work with him every day?" Helena asked.

"Hmm..." Alice slid into one of the wrought iron chairs and rested her chin on her fist. "No, that pretty much sums him up. He's smart, knows his stuff, and he's dependable."

"Which are also good qualities," Julia agreed.

Ruby's phone buzzed. "It's Lawrence," she reported, stifling a giggle.

"What does Law have to say?" Alice asked.

"Is he feeling better?" Helena and Julia asked in unison.

Ruby showed them the picture of Lawrence's close-up photo of his blood shot eyes.

"Oh my. What happened?" Julia asked.

"He's asking if that is a side effect of the soup I left him." Ruby replied with a text. "FYI, it's not."

"Alice, look at that," Julia directed. "Is that a reaction of some sort?"

Alice shook her head. "Lawrence's eyes always get like that when he has a serious allergy fit. He's just giving Slop a hard time."

Another text came through and Ruby's face sobered a bit and her hand hesitated a moment over the phone before she sent a quick response.

"What else did he say?" Helena asked, concerned at her friend's change in mood.

Ruby forced a smile. "Oh, he was just wishing me well tonight on my date with Jimmy."

She felt Julia's penetrative stare as she feigned nonchalance and smiled in greeting to the waiter approaching their table. She didn't know why it bothered her that Lawrence felt completely okay with her dating Jimmy. It's not like they had a relationship beyond friendship. Not like she wanted one, either. But for some odd reason, she'd thought Lawrence, or any of the brothers really, would have put up an argument of some sort. But none of them had. *That was a good thing*, she thought. It meant they liked Jimmy, and it's hard to receive that sort of acceptance from *all* the Hastings brothers. And yet, Ruby found herself a little disappointed they, or Lawrence, didn't even blink an eye.

The afternoon was a delightful day. Beautiful weather, a day off work, time with girlfriends she'd craved to have in her life, and yet she felt excitement for her date slowly waning. She startled as Julia tapped her arm. Alice and Helena were nowhere in sight, and Ruby glanced around in surprise.

"Welcome back."

"Where did they go?" Ruby asked.

"Helena wanted to look at the jewelry in Reese's over there." Julia pointed across the street. "You okay?"

"Fine." Ruby answered a little too quickly and she shriveled under Julia's sympathetic gaze.

"Nervous?"

"Not really. I'm sure it will be fun."

"Then what is it? Was Lawrence rude in his other text?"

"No." Ruby sighed and placed her face in her hands before rubbing them over her short-cropped hair. "You'll think I'm crazy."

"Try me."

"Is it weird I'm a little disappointed the brothers aren't giving me more of a tough time over dating Jimmy?"

"You expected them to?"

"Well, yeah. Anyone I've ever dated they've interfered somehow. And this time, it's like they don't even notice or care, really. Which—" She paused a moment. "I know is a good thing. Only shows they like Jimmy. But still, it just feels weird that I'm not hearing *something* about it from one of them. I mean, for Lawrence to wish me well is so weird."

Julia squeezed her hand. "Consider it a blessing. And they may seem fine with it right now, but if things were to progress and grow serious, I'm sure they'll start giving you a hard time."

"It's weird that I'm missing that, huh?"

Julia laughed. "Not at all. I imagine it is like waiting for the other shoe to drop. You know it's coming, but you don't know when. And they're nice right now... what is that about?"

"Exactly." Ruby laughed with her and was thankful someone understood.

"Well, enjoy it while it lasts. I think Jimmy seems nice. And I hope, for your sake, that it is a fun evening. You deserve a night out."

"Thanks."

"And you deserve a man who appreciates you and wants to treat you special."

Ruby glanced at her watch. "I guess we better get a move on if I'm going to have time to shower and take too long getting ready."

Julia laughed. "Don't worry about Porter. He can stay with us tonight. Waylon will enjoy the company." She stood and Ruby followed her towards Helena's car where Alice and Helena waited.

"Any luck?" Julia asked.

"I found a darling bracelet." Helena held up the small gift bag from the jewelry store as Alice rolled her eyes.

"Only Helena could use the word darling and get by with it."

Ruby climbed into the back seat with Alice as Julia and Helena slid up front. "Thanks for today, guys." Ruby draped her dress over her lap.

"It was fun," Helena chimed. "We need to do it more often."

"And we will. Thursday," Alice added. "In the meantime—" She paused and glanced at a text from Calvin. "Oh no. Hobbs injured his back leg."

"Hobbs?" Helena asked.

"Calvin's puppy. Cal says Hobbs was being nosy in the shop and knocked over a pile of parts onto himself. Hold on, let me check on this." She requested a photo. "Not too bad. He probably just bruised it. But Cal has gotten attached to that little booger. The dog sneezes and Cal thinks he's got Parvo."

"It's sweet." Julia smiled. "Graham's gotten rather attached to Waylon. Even let him sleep in the house the other night. When I walked over in the morning for coffee, Waylon wasn't outside. He was draped in Graham's recliner."

"Oh wow." Ruby's eyes widened. "That is big."

"Right?!" Julia laughed.

"Porter unfortunately spends most of his day with Randy on the porch of the diner. He doesn't seem to mind, and believe it or not, Randy is quite the dog whisperer." Ruby adjusted the sleeve of her shirt as she shifted in her seat.

"What made you decide to name him Porter?" Julia asked.

Ruby smirked. "When we were kids, Lawrence and I would pretend we were Porter Wagoner and Dolly Parton. We'd pretend the haybarn was the Grand Ole Opry. Hayes and Seth were always our audience or band members. Anyways, Lawrence told me he named his puppy Dolly, so naturally she needed a Porter to be her friend."

"That's really cute." Julia placed a hand on her heart. "I can't imagine Lawrence pretending to be Porter Wagoner."

"Hayes would sing for him and Lawrence would lip sync." Ruby laughed. "You remember that, Al?" Ruby asked.

"I do remember stumbling upon a few of your concerts back then." She grinned. "Y'all were filthy, hay sticking out of your hair and covered in dirt, but you still sang your hearts out. And danced," she added.

"Does Lawrence still dance?" Helena asked on a

laugh.

"I have no idea." Ruby laughed, her heart warming at the memories made with Lawrence. Out of all the brothers, most of her memories involved him. Hayes as well, but mostly Lawrence. He'd always been there for her. Good and bad, no matter the circumstances, he was her rock. She still remembered the days that her grandparents passed away. Lawrence was the first person she'd called. He was the first brother to come see about her. And he'd stayed with her. Cooked for her. Held her while she cried. Helped her clean up the diner when she'd moved back to Parks from masseuse school. She was grateful for him. She was grateful for all the Hastings brothers. And looking at her friends in the car, she was thankful that her friendship with the Hastings family led to even more wonderful friendships with the amazing women they'd chosen.

∞

"What are you doing out here?" Hayes leaned out of his open truck window as Lawrence lifted his welding helmet and swiped his sleeve over his nose.

"Workin'. What does it look like?"

"I thought you were on strict orders to rest today."

"I got bored. Besides, I'm the welder. Would make

sense for me to look the pipe pens over before Clint starts cutting."

"And I thought that was postponed until tomorrow?" Hayes narrowed his eyes at his brother.

"Stop coddling," Lawrence growled.

Hayes smirked. "Not coddlin', just makin' an observation. If you need rest, take it. The pens can wait."
"I'm fine. Besides, I've got a lot on my mind. I don't want to be sittin' around the house stewing."

"This about Slop's date with the vet tech?"

"What?" Lawrence's head snapped up. "No."

Hayes's face split into a knowing smile. "You sure?"

"Why would that bother me? Ruby deserves to be treated to a night out."

"I agree. I just thought it might bug you, you two always being close and all."

"Nope. Doesn't bother me." Lawrence grabbed a piece of pipe off the ground and tossed it with a little more force than necessary to the discard pile.

"Right. Well, if you start feeling worse, go home," Hayes warned. "I need your help at the stables this week and I'd rather you be on your game instead of sneezing every five minutes."

"Got it." Lawrence lowered his welding helmet and turned back to the pens, Hayes taking the signal and slowly driving up the dirt road towards his house.

It didn't bother Lawrence that Ruby was going on a date with Jimmy. He was happy for her, really. She'd given so much of her time to the diner, he was glad she finally had the opportunity to take a night off. Now, if Jimmy turned out to be a jerk, Lawrence would have a problem. A big problem. But the guy seemed nice enough. Was it weird to think of Ruby dating? Yes. But it was also weird that Graham was head over heels for Julia, Cal smitten with Al, and Philip drooling over Helena. Lots of weird the last several months. So why not toss Sloppy into the mix? He hadn't dated in a long while. As he thought about it, he could only pinpoint one woman over the last year or so. Pretty pitiful results, if he was honest with himself. But he hadn't made it a priority. Much like his other brothers. He liked his life the way it was. He enjoyed the company of his brothers and their women. He enjoyed Annie and Henry. And he enjoyed hanging out at the diner with the locals. He didn't quite see the point in muddying that up with a woman in his life. He flirted with some single women here and there, but he wasn't looking for anything serious.

He held the torch over the pipe, sparks flying as he cut through the seam enough to wiggle the rusted-out pipe from its position and tossed it aside. He heard another truck approaching and saw Clint pulling up, Graham riding alongside him in the passenger side. Now that was a rare combination.

"You're making me look bad, Law." Clint hopped out. "We weren't going to work on this until you were back to being sunshine and rainbows."

"Figured I could get started." He nodded towards Graham.

"Well, suns about down, so call it a day." Graham stated, leaning across the center console so as to be heard, his eyes already surveying the amount of work Lawrence had accomplished the last few hours.

"Yeah, that's my last pipe for today." Lawrence removed his welding helmet from his head and tossed it onto the bed of his truck. "Think I'm going to head into town. Eat at Annie's."

"It is Friday," Clint pointed out. "She'd be disappointed if you didn't."

"Don't get them sick," Graham warned.

"I won't. It's just allergies."

"Still. I'd rather you didn't eat there," Graham continued. "Go to Slop's and get a meal."

"She's not there," Lawrence reminded him. "She's got a date with Jimmy."

"So?" Clint shrugged. "Sal is still in the kitchen and that hot dancer is the new waitress."

"Dancer?" Lawrence asked.

Clint grinned. "Yeah, Ruby hired an exotic dancer as her new waitress."

"What?" Lawrence's eyes widened in surprise.

Graham held up his hand. "Be nice. She's trying to get out of a bad situation, and Ruby is giving her a chance. You'll treat her with respect."

"I am," Clint defended. "Just pointing out that she's hot."

Lawrence shook his head. "I'll talk to Annie. If she doesn't want me around, then the diner it is. I just don't feel like cooking. And I'm done eating that awful soup Ruby brought over."

"The cure-all?" Graham asked.

Lawrence nodded as Clint cringed and shuttered. "Yeah, that stuff is terrible," Clint concurred. "It works though."

"Well, pack it in." Graham nodded his farewell as Clint slid back behind the wheel and began to drive away.

He liked working the ranch. There was nothing better than putting a good, long day in on the land. Seeing the fruits of your labor as the seasons turned. Not only that, Lawrence loved working the land with his brothers. His grandparents, God rest 'em, had left a legacy for him and his brothers. His parents as well. He didn't feel obligated to follow in their footsteps, he felt honored. It was the life he'd always wanted. There was no contemplation to ever leave Parks, not even for college. His life, his work, his love was working his family's land, and he hoped he would always have the privilege. There was a peace in knowing what it was you were meant to do. He knew Clint struggled with that very dilemma at the moment. Philip had in the past and had eventually found his place. So it was only a matter of time before Clint did as well. Lawrence, however, always knew his place. It was here. The 7H was his. It was all of theirs to hold onto, to groom, to prune, to develop, to keep. He wanted to raise his family here, give his children the opportunity to love the land as much as he did. One day. Until then, he climbed into the truck and briefly rested his congested head on the steering wheel. Until then, he'd continue his Friday tradition and eat with Annie and Henry or at the diner. His stomach released a low, rumbling growl offering its sentiments of being abused by the "cure-all" all morning. He turned the key in the ignition, "And that's a wrap for today," he mumbled, directing his wheels towards Parks.

H

Chapter Three

Ruby fidgeted and adjusted the shoulder of her dress as she awaited her food at the fast food chain restaurant. She felt a bit overdressed compared to the place and compared to Jimmy, who sported a pair of worn jeans and a light blue t-shirt. Had she thought his invite to dinner meant a nice restaurant in Fort Stockton? Yes. Was she a little disappointed that it was a drive-in burger joint in Sheffield? Yes. However, Jimmy seemed to appreciate the effort she'd made in her appearance and the evening was fun despite the odd looks she received every now and then. The teenager cashier brought the basket containing her burger and fries over to the booth and slid it in front of her while plopping down ketchup packets before scurrying back behind the register.

Jimmy, not losing a beat in his conversation as he spoke about his childhood, grabbed a couple of packets and began doctoring up his burger.

Ruby wasn't really in the mood for a burger, so she picked at her fries for a few minutes while she listened. Food was a funny thing for her. She was around it 24/7, so she rarely had an appetite. And when she did, it was for meals she didn't prepare at the diner— like Annie's pot roast or potato soup or Julia's creamy chicken pasta. But a burger and fries just wasn't cutting it for her tonight, especially since she'd had her heart set on a chicken parmesan or seafood supper in Fort Stockton. She didn't blame Jimmy for her disappointment. He'd never actually said where he planned to take her. It was her own fault for reading too much into his offer. She hadn't been on a date in so long, it felt nice getting all dressed up for a night out regardless of the destination. And Sal, true to his word, hadn't contacted her or interrupted her evening with calls from the diner. Ruby would admit she was a bit nervous leaving her new hire, Zoe, on her own, but she needed to branch out sooner or later, and there was no better time than now. She was in good hands with Sal anyway.

"So Roly is my pal now. I'm thankful Alice is cool with me having him at her house. Not a lot of landlords are."

Missing his conversation, Ruby nodded, knowing at least that Roly was his pet. She assumed dog or cat, but perhaps he had a ferret. Jimmy looked like the kind of guy who'd own a ferret. Quirky, fun, and a bit eccentric. "I'm glad that's worked out for you. Cal put a lot of work into that house."

"I can tell. I saw some pictures of the before." He grimaced. "Can't believe Alice lived there."

Ruby laughed. "Yeah, well, Alice doesn't really *live* anywhere. She just sleeps places."

Jimmy nodded. "I've started to get that." He took a sip of his drink. "So what about you? You have the house on the corner of main street, right? That's a pretty big house."

"It belonged to my grandparents," Ruby explained.

"Ah. The diner did as well, right?"

"Yep." Her smile softened. "They raised me. Well, along with Annie, Henry, and the Hastings family."

"Yeah, I've noticed all of you are close. I mean, I get it, they're a big family, but I just didn't understand how close knit everyone in this town was until now."

She tilted her head. "Is it weird?"

He laughed. "Sometimes, but mostly at work. Alice and Julia talk about the brothers *all* the time. And I like the guys, don't get me wrong, but I know more about them based on my conversations at work than I do from actually getting to know them. So that's a bit weird at times."

"The brothers are pretty laid-back. They know Alice talks smack about them behind their backs, lovingly so, and Julia is so overly in love with Graham, she's excited to learn anything and everything about the entire family right now." Ruby gave a small giggle. "Which is actually sweet to see that Graham has such a woman in his life. If you'd grown up with Graham Hastings, you'd know how big a feat Julia's accomplished."

"I'm beginning to understand the more I get to know him."

"But they're all kind and loving in their own ways. Graham takes care of those he loves. Sometimes with a bit more vigor than necessary. Cal serves the ones he loves. He is constantly seeing how he can help someone. Philip is the best listener out of the bunch. Annie will tell you that is his spiritual gift."

"And the others?"

Ruby leaned back in her chair and sighed. "Lawrence loves through laughter. He loves making people laugh. Hayes will bend over backwards to help someone, much like Cal. Clint protects those he loves. He's a bit rough around the edges, similar to Graham, though don't ever tell the two of them that. And Seth, he's just a ray of sunshine. He's there to brighten your day, even when you weren't aware that you needed it."

"Wow." Jimmy inhaled a deep breath. "Sounds like they hung the moon."

Ruby laughed. "Far from it. Graham can be rude and borderline mean when he wants to be. Cal can be intrusive, Philip can be nosy, Lawrence is one of the most stubborn people you'll meet, Hayes can be spacey, Clint can be arrogant, and Seth can be annoying." She shrugged her shoulders. "It's a balance only they can pull off, it seems."

"I don't hear much negative these days at the clinic. Though Alice will vent every now and then when she needs her space."

"We all need to vent sometimes, especially when it comes to the people we love. We love them, but as with all things, sometimes the people and things we love annoy us."

"True. So, you were a masseuse before working at the diner, right?"

"Not quite. I was in school to become one. I never finished."

"Ever thought about going back?"

"Not really." She nudged her barely touched dinner to the side.

"Why not? Do you plan on staying in Parks forever?"

"Maybe. I'm not really sure. There for a while I was contemplating leaving. But it's home. And it's where my family is at."

"They're not really your family, though."

His comment stung, and had his face held any sort of animosity she would have lost her temper. But his gaze held nonchalance. He didn't understand the connection between her and the Hastings family or with Annie and Henry. He'd talked about how close his family was and his siblings. His circumstances were different. His family was different. And from an outsider's perspective, she could see how her relationship with the brothers was a bit odd. But they were her family, and always would be. "Actually, they are," she said simply, and was thankful he left it at that.

"Well," He stood. "you ready to head back to Parks?"

"Sure." She grabbed her beaded handbag and stood, thankful she hadn't spilled or stained her new dress and already contemplating returning it to the store. She'd spent more on this dress than she'd normally spend on an outfit, thinking it was for a special night out. A little disappointed, she was thankful she'd kept the receipt.

∞

"Good to see ya'." Sal reached across the bar and shook Lawrence's hand. "'Fraid Slop ain't here. She's got a date with that animal doc that lives out back."

"So I heard." Lawrence nodded towards the new waitress. "How's she workin' out?"

"Pretty good. Got a good head on her shoulders. Seems to have caught on pretty quick. I've only had to come out here twice to lay down the law."

"What do you mean?"

"Oh, between her and Ruby there's always some rowdy cowboy or roughneck trying to make a move."

"I'm glad you're here to see about them, Sal."

The big man shrugged and nodded towards the kitchen. "I better get back behind the stove. I'll fry you up a steak. You look completely wore out, boy."

"Haven't been feeling so hot the last couple of days."

"A steak will fix you right up. Kara!" He yelled and waved the new waitress over. "Get this man a sweet tea, will ya?"

She complied quickly and placed it on the bar in front of Lawrence. Smiling, she grabbed the notepad from her apron. "Is there anything else I can get you?"

Lawrence pointed towards Sal's retreating back. "He's got me taken care of. Lawrence, by the way." He extended his hand. "Lawrence Hastings."

Her eyes acknowledged his name before she did. "Another brother, hm? There seems to be a few of you around here."

"Just a few."

"Kara. Nice to meet you. Ruby's tried to educate me on all of you and said I'd be seeing you all sooner or later."

"We're here a lot. How you like workin' at Sloppy's?

She seemed surprised by the question, as if no one asked her such a simple thing. "Oh, it's great. I mean, I still have a lot to learn, but Ruby's been kind to me and so has Sal. I think I could like it here."

"Good. You live here in Parks?"

"No. Not yet. I live in Sheffield."

"Parks is better," Lawrence pointed out.

She grinned. "I'm starting to see that too. The people have been very welcoming."

"Lawrence Dean!" A female voice called from the doorway of the diner and footsteps tapped towards him. He immediately knew who it was because only one formidable woman ever called him by his middle name. He turned to find Annie standing in the doorway, her hands on her hips. "Now, I know you don't feel well, but that is no excuse not to come by for supper and stand me up."

Kara's brows lifted as if she were trying to figure out Lawrence's relationship with the older woman.

"I talked to Henry earlier. Did he not tell you?"

"Just now." Annie huffed, plopping onto the stool beside him. "After I made a giant batch of fried deer cutlets."

"That sounds awesome."

"It is. And Philip, Helena, and Seth are all eating your portion."

"And why are you not there?"

"I came to check on you." Her voice softened as she surveyed him with a motherly gaze. "You seem alright to me." She swatted his arm. "Which just makes me madder."

He chuckled as he draped his arm around her shoulders and gave her a light squeeze. "I didn't want to bring my germs to your house, Annie."

"Honey, I helped raise you. You and your brothers are walking germs and I am immune." She looked up at Kara. "Hi there, Sweetie, I don't think we've met, but I've heard all about you from Ruby. You must be Kara."

"Yes ma'am." Kara's nervous reply had Annie chuckling.

"Oh, don't worry, honey, I'm not going to lash out at you too. Though you are welcome to come by on Friday evenings and eat as well when you don't have to work." Annie turned her attention back to Lawrence. "Have you heard from Ruby?"

"No ma'am. She's on her date."

"I know that, but I figured she'd text you and let you know how it's going."

"Why would she do that?"

"Because she's your Ruby, dimwit." Annie rolled her eyes. "Honestly, Lawrence, are you sure you feel okay?"

"She is not *my* Ruby." Lawrence looked up in relief as Sal walked out of the kitchen with a large platter piled high with food and set it before him.

"Oh, hogwash. You two were inseparable as kids and you're good friends now. If she needed a date escape, you'd be the first person she'd call."

"Well, she didn't, so I guess it went well."

Kara ducked away to go check on other customers for a moment before walking back behind the bar and wiping down the counter.

"I wonder if she's having a good time," Annie fretted. "Sweet girl deserves to be treated to a nice night out."

"I agree." Lawrence took an oversized bite of green beans and kept his head down above his plate.

Annie eyed him with a narrowed gaze before the bell above the diner door gave a small chime. Ruby walked inside, carrying her small, beaded handbag clutched in her hands. Her eyes landed on Lawrence and then Annie.

"Well." Annie placed a hand over her heart as she hopped off her stool and intercepted Ruby. "Honey, you look gorgeous." She gave Ruby a small spin. "Lawrence, look at her."

Lawrence briefly glanced up and then back at his place, his eyes immediately bouncing back up to Ruby. "Wow." He turned on his stool and smiled. "Lookin' good, Slop."

She flushed. "Thanks. I better sneak home and change before I stain it. I plan on returning it tomorrow."

"Why would you return such a beautiful dress?" Annie asked.

Lawrence then saw the disappointment on Ruby's face and knew her date had not gone according to plan. Though he felt upset for her, part of him was relieved. That was new.

"Oh, it was expensive, and I... I just don't need it."

Annie caught on to the disappointed tone too and flashed Lawrence another narrowed gaze.

He looked at Ruby. "Don't return the dress, Slop. It suits you."

"Thanks, Lawrence."

"Suits her?" Annie stood to the side of Ruby, her arm around her slim waist. "Lawrence Dean, this woman is stunning in this dress. Step up your game, son."

Ruby and Lawrence both laughed.

"She's right. My apologies. You look phenomenal, Ruby. Keep it." He turned back to his food as Kara topped off his glass.

"How's it going tonight?" Ruby asked the waitress.

"Good. Quiet, thankfully." She smiled shyly as if ashamed of previous nights' events.

"That's what I like to hear. This one hasn't been giving you trouble, has he?" She nodded her head towards Lawrence.

"Not at all." Kara smiled. "Another Hastings brother to continue their good reputation."

"She obviously hasn't met Clint yet, has she?" Lawrence asked and had all the women laughing.

"Oh, she did, but he just gawked at her the whole time," Ruby explained as Kara's cheeks flamed pink.

"A beautiful woman comes to town and men lose their heads." Annie released her hold on Ruby. "I better get on back to the house, seeing as I have company and all." She glowered at Lawrence before turning her attention back to Ruby. "You hungry, sweetie?"

"She just had a date, Annie." Lawrence rolled his eyes.

"Starving, actually." Ruby replied, to everyone's surprise.

"Well, then you come on and take ol' Henry's breath away with your lovely dress and I'll feed ya some deer steak and scalloped potatoes. You get well, Lawrence. No more missing meals."

"Yes ma'am." He watched as Annie and Ruby had their own private conversation before Annie walked out of the diner. Ruby came to the bar and sat a moment longer. "You not goin' to Annie's?"

"I am in a few minutes. How are you feeling?"

"Better for the most part. Still have some sniffles but overall okay."

"Good."

"I take it the date didn't go well?"

"It wasn't bad."

"Wasn't bad is not the same as good," Lawrence replied.

"No, you're right about that. Jimmy's nice and we talked a lot, which was good."

"Where'd he take you to eat? That new seafood place in Fort Stockton?"

"No. We went to Sheffield."

"Sheffield?" Lawrence asked. "What place in Sheffield?"

Ruby's cheeks blushed as she muttered, "Bargain Burger."

Lawrence's back snapped straight. "Bargain Burger!"

She placed a restraining hand on his arm. "Shhh, Law. Not so loud."

"Dressed like that?" He nodded to her dress. "He took you to Bargain Burger?"

"Yes, now let's just drop it."

"Alright, I officially hate the guy."

Ruby chuckled. "No. Don't. It was my own fault for reading too much into the dinner invite."

"No, it isn't. And even if he'd originally planned to take you to Bargain Burger, when he got an eyeful of you in that dress, a smart man would have diverted his path to Fort Stockton and taken you somewhere nice."

"Thanks." She adjusted the sleeve on the dress as she sighed. "It's okay though. It was a nice break regardless."

"You going to see him again?"

"If he asks."

"Bargain Burger," Lawrence muttered in distaste as he took a bite of his steak. "I feel like I should punch him for being so stupid. I mean, I'm not much of the dating type, but even I know not to take you to Bargain Burger."

Kara swiped the counter in front of them and shared a small smile with Ruby at his comment.

"Well," Ruby slapped him on the back. "maybe one day you can treat me to a nice seafood dinner, Law. I'll even wear this dress." She laughed as she stood. "I'm headed to Annie's. You good here?" she asked Kara.

"Yep."

"Don't let this one pester you too long." Ruby rested her head on Lawrence's shoulder a minute before grabbing her purse. "Rest, Lawrence. Eat more of the 'cure-all.'"

"Over my dead body."

Laughing, she walked to the door and outside. He stared after her a moment, thankful that he'd cheered her up somewhat.

"You know, I don't think she'd say no if you *did* ask her to a nice seafood dinner in Fort Stockton," Kara said in a low tone.

Lawrence turned back towards the bar and shook his head. "Slop and I are better off as friends. She deserves someone better than me."

"That's sweet." Kara reached for his glass and he waved her off. "If there is one thing I've learned since being here at the diner, it's how much your family loves her. She's told me a little bit of her story, and I think it's wonderful how your family treats her."

"*My* family?" Lawrence shook his head. "Ruby *is* my family. She has been since we were kids. There's no special treatment on our end. We aren't saints. If anything, she's the saint for putting up with us."

"Which, again, is very sweet." Kara slipped his empty plate away and walked it towards the kitchen. She came back to an empty barstool and a wad of cash tossed on the bar top.

H

Chapter Four

Keeping busy was easy.

Ruby was used to the hectic schedule of the diner. In fact, she spent more time at the diner than she did her own home. On Sunday afternoons, after church and the traditional family meal at Annie's house, she'd come to the diner to deep clean the floors, scrub surfaces, wrap silverware, restock supplies, and make sure she had enough ingredients and supplies in the kitchen for Sal for the upcoming week. She'd go over receipts and numbers for the week. She'd calculate her goals and expectations for the following week's business, and she'd even treat herself to a soda while contemplating what new items she could possibly add to the menu, though she rarely made changes there.

But this Sunday was different. Instead of a quiet diner to herself, Kara sat across from her wrapping silverware in napkins as well. The new waitress took a sip of her soda and sighed. "I'm pretty sure there is nothing better than that first sip of carbonation."

Ruby grinned. "I strongly agree."

"Thanks again for the job, Ruby. I've loved working here so far."

"I'm just thankful you came on board. The other night I went to bed at 8:30. I can't tell you the last time I was in bed before midnight. It was glorious." Ruby laughed. "And I was able to go on a date. Which, I'm pretty sure it's been even longer since I've done that."

"Well, I hope I can continue to help you out. I'm free any day or time, even Sundays," she pointed out.

"The diner is always closed on Sundays, but it is when I come in and do stuff like this if I don't have time to during the week. But Sunday mornings are always church and then Annie's. You should come with me next week."

Kara fidgeted the fork and knife in her hand. "Oh. Um... I would, but... I'm not sure people would really like me there. Considering what I used to do."

Ruby set aside her napkin roll. "If that's the case then no one should be at church." She laughed. "You don't have to be perfect to go to church, Kara. We all have pasts. Some worse than others. Church should be the first place imperfect people should feel welcome. But if you don't want to, believe me, I get it. But the next best place to church is around Annie and Henry's picnic table. Even if you don't join us for church, I know she would absolutely love it if you joined us for the big Sunday meal."

"She did mention that the other day. Well... for a Friday."

"Ah." Ruby nodded. "That's when she feeds a few of us as well. Either one, you're more than welcome. It's nice to have friends in Parks."

"I appreciate the offer. I'll think about it." Kara took another sip of her soda. "So, do you plan on going on another date with Jimmy? I noticed he was hanging out at the bar last night."

"If he asks." Ruby nodded.

"Well, that doesn't sound very exciting," Kara laughed.

Ruby's lips tilted. "I mean, yes, I guess."

"Even worse."

Ruby tossed a wadded-up napkin at her. "Alright, yes. I would say yes if he asked. But I don't know if he will. He seems content with keeping our relationship how it already is."

"A casual flirtation over a bar top?"

"Pretty much."

"Can I ask you something?"

"Sure."

Kara studied her a moment. "If one of the Hastings brothers were to ask you on a date, would you say yes?"

Ruby guffawed. "Now that would be the day. And which do you suppose would do the askin'?"

Kara shrugged. "I don't know. I was just curious."

"Well, I don't see that day coming any time soon, but speaking of those boys, I'm headed out to the ranch after we're done. Want to come with?"

"I better not. Not if I'm to get back to Sheffield and then be here in the morning."

"Just stay with me," Ruby invited. "In fact, you're more than welcome to crash here during the week, too, if you're ever too tired to drive home. I've got plenty of room."

"Really?"

"Yeah." Ruby stood to her feet and bent over to pick up the bin of silverware. Walking it behind the bar, she intercepted Kara and took her drink to the sink in the kitchen. "I'm going to fix a drink for the road. Want one?"

Nodding, Kara waited out front and Ruby hurried back and forth, jingling her keys when she walked back into the dining room. "I've got to pick up Porter at Julia's, so we'll have a dog riding with us on the way back. Hope that's okay."

"I'm good with that."

"Then let's go." Ruby unlocked her car and both women headed out to the 7H. The drive was as familiar as the steps into her own house, and she could drive it blindfolded if need be. Though, maybe that wasn't quite the best analogy considering she and Lawrence had tried just that when they were sixteen and crashed Cal's truck in the ditch. The memory made her smile as she turned through the front entrance, the iron lettering welcoming them to the property.

"Wow," Kara mumbled as Graham's white house came into view. "It's beautiful."

"That's where Graham lives." Ruby pointed to the small house next door. "Julia and Alice are currently living in the guest house."

"That's a guest house? That's way bigger than my little apartment."

"Graham wanted space for at least four people to feel comfortable. It's a two-bedroom house. I'll have to take you inside. Julia has decorated it a bit more, but it was beautiful to begin with." She parked her car in front of Graham's house and Julia stepped out onto the porch and waved. "That's Julia."

Ruby and Kara climbed out, Julia's smile widening at the sight of a new face.

"Well, look at the queen of the castle." Ruby placed both hands on her hips and studied Julia. "It suits you."

Laughing, Julia waved away her comment. "I was just about to head down to the creek near Cal's. The guys are there with the dogs."

"That's why I'm here, though Porter will be sad to leave."

"Give me a second and I'll grab my tennis shoes and walk with you." Julia darted back into the house as Alice stepped out of the guest house, lowering her sunglasses. She was dressed in a pair of daisy duke shorts and a bikini top.

"I thought that was you pulling up, Slop. Who's your friend?"

"This is Kara."

"Ah, the new waitress." Alice shook her hand. "I've heard a lot about you."

Julia hustled out of Graham's house, carrying a tumbler of tea for herself as she met them in the yard. They all fell into step with one another.

"I'm Julia, by the way." She leaned forward a bit to smile at Kara.

"Kara. Nice to meet you."

"Oh." Julia's brows rose. "You're the woman we can thank for getting Ruby out of that diner and on a hot date."

Ruby laughed. "Hot might be an overstatement." Having filled them in on the date with Jimmy at Annie's over lunch, Julia's determination to unite Jimmy and Ruby on another date had not abated.

"Well, the next one will be."

The sound of barking and men yelling and laughing came from behind Cal's house as they walked up.

"The men have been camped out at this creek ever since those rains a few weeks ago. Enjoying the water while it lasts, which won't be much longer with this heat lately," Alice reported.

As they rounded the side of the house, her face split into a radiant smile at the sight of Calvin standing in the creek, his back to them. She took off in a sprint straight for him, launching herself onto his back. He stumbled a few steps before he realized who'd grabbed him and quicker than swatting a fly, had whipped Alice off his back and into his arms, dipping her into a long, steamy kiss.

"Whoa." Ruby fanned herself.

"And to think they didn't think they had chemistry." Julia shook her head in pity. "Good thing I came along to help them realize it."

Kara chuckled and had Julia wriggling her eyebrows.

Hayes, lay on the bank of the creek on his back, resting on his elbows, the filtered sunlight teasing his facel opened one eye and smiled up at them. "Ladies."

Ruby ruffled his hair in response. His gaze landed on Kara and he sat upright. "And who's this?" He ran a quick hand through his hair, as if realizing he didn't wear a hat to tip to the newcomer.

"This is Kara," Ruby explained.

"Ah, the infamous Kara." He smiled in welcome. "Nice to meet you. I'm Hayes Hastings."

"Nice to meet you as well." She shook his outstretched hand. "You're the horse brother, right?"

He beamed proudly. "That's me. You like horses?"

"Doesn't every woman like horses?"

"That is a very good point." Hayes chuckled. "Well, if you ride, you're welcome at the stables any time. We've got some pretty docile mares that make good riding companions." He trailed off as he saw Julia standing next to her and remembered his future sister-in-law did not have a good experience on the back of one of his most docile horses.

"Don't tip-toe around me." Julia patted his shoulder. "Those were extenuating circumstances. And without that horrible experience, I would not have grown closer to Graham as quickly."

"What happened?" Kara asked.

"Have a seat, I'll tell ya." Hayes patted the ground next to him, Kara looking to Ruby for approval. Ruby nodded that she was totally fine with her hanging out with Hayes. In fact, Ruby knew the brother would ease some of Kara's anxiety of being around unfamiliar faces. The poor woman considered herself a red mark on society due to her previous work as an exotic dancer. Ruby was determined to help change that.

She walked toward the water's edge and saw Lawrence and Seth standing in the creek. Lawrence, shirtless, was scrubbing an unwilling Porter with a bar of soap. He wrestled with the young pup as it whined to be released to play with his friends, but Lawrence held tight, receiving a bath of licks to the face and enough soap on himself to qualify for cleanliness. His arms, tense and toned, held onto the dog's middle as he scrubbed Porter's face and behind his ears. She admired the view a minute, not realizing Lawrence hid such musculature beneath his wardrobe of plaid shirts. He was definitely not the sixteen-year-old boy she drove around town with anymore. He looked up and grinned as Porter licked the side of his face.

"I owe you," she called out.

"Not really. He and Dolly decided to roll in a dead armadillo. It was more out of necessity." He dipped the dog's body in the water, Porter kicking his legs to swim away as Lawrence rinsed his face off and released him. Porter darted towards Ruby. She held out her hand to keep him from jumping up at her while he was soaked, but he was too excited and planted wet paws on the front of her shirt. Too pleased that she had such a loving companion, she wasn't angry, but instead gave him a loving rub behind the ears and kissed his nose.

Lawrence waded towards the bank and climbed out of the water, his wet jeans sagging a bit on his narrow hips. Her heart ticked up a beat as he flashed his signature smile.

"You look like you feel better."

"I do. Like night and day from yesterday. Almost 100 percent." He replied.

"Good. I'm glad."

"Glad to see you invited her out." Lawrence nodded towards Kara talking with Hayes, the woman relaxed and laughing at whatever Hayes was telling her.

"I think she was a bit nervous."

"Hayes is a good one for her to talk with, then."

"Yep. I thought so too."

Lawrence nodded towards the water. "You getting in?"

She looked at her clothes. "I'm not exactly dressed for the creek."

"So? Neither was I."

"I think I'll just hang out over here." Ruby pointed to the grass.

Shrugging, Lawrence started walking back out into the water. Ruby turned to head back towards Hayes and Kara when a pair of strong hands plucked her up off the grass and tossed her over a bare shoulder. She squealed. "Lawrence Dean, you better put me down this instant!"

Everyone watched as she beat his rear as her face dipped closer to the water beneath them. Lawrence kept walking. "Lawrence!" Ruby yelled. "I mean it!"

Seth hurried towards them in the creek and Ruby reached out for the lifeline, only for him to drag his arms through the water sending a tidal wave right at her head. She covered her face as everyone laughed. She kicked her legs, but Lawrence's death grip held her firm.

"Graham! Graham, help me!"

Clint mimicked her cry for help across the creek as he laughed. Graham and Julia watched, the eldest brother not coming to her rescue.

"Cal!" Ruby called. "Anybody?! Seriously, Law. I don't want to get soaked. This is my only pair of clothes." She tried to appeal to his sensibilities.

When he reached the middle of the creek, she felt his hold on her waist loosen and she gripped his sides so as not to tip over. His hands slid to beneath her feet.

"Better let go, Ruby." He laughed.

"No way."

"Seth," Lawrence called his younger brother over. "Tickle her."

Ruby writhed in his arms. "No. Okay, no. No. I'll let go." She released her hold on Lawrence's hips and felt him lift her straight into the air by her feet and pushing her up and out. She screamed as she soared and then landed in the cool water.

∞

Lawrence, pleased with himself, stood with his hands on his hips while Ruby's arms flailed as she tried to regain composure after her splash. She pushed water his direction, the sprinkles that actually hit him not phasing him in the slightest. "You're a horrible man, Lawrence Hastings."

"So they tell me." He grinned as he pointed to Graham and Julia. "You ready for a swim, Jewels?"

"No, thank you. I prefer being right here." She slid her arm around Graham's waist for added security, knowing full well Lawrence wouldn't dare touch her under his brother's protection. What none of them were expecting, was Graham's quick reflexes of scooping Julia into his arms and tossing her out into the middle of the creek. Her scream resounded and gurgled as she hit the water.

Alice lost it and laughed hysterically as Julia emerged sputtering in shock. "Graham!" Julia looked to him in complete horror and betrayal, which made everyone laugh harder. "I can't believe you just did that." She tried to push back her wet hair from her face, and even sopping wet, was one of the most beautiful women in the world. Graham's lips twitched before a heavy shove on his back sent him stumbling off the edge of the bank into the water, boots and all. Seth sprinted out of arms reach before his oldest brother could retaliate.

Lawrence extended a helping hand to Julia to help her claim her footing. "Thank you, Lawrence." She stood in the creek, making attempts at straightening her appearance.

"Just stop it, Julia." Alice splashed her friend with water. "Accept defeat."

"You two coming?" Ruby called to Hayes and Kara.

Hayes stood to his feet and helped Kara to hers. "I don't know if I want to look like a wet rat around company."

Lawrence watched Clint sneak up behind his brother, inch by quiet inch. Hayes stood with his hands on his hips and just when Clint went in for the kill, Hayes ducked and spun, using Clint's momentum against himself and hurdled his brother over his shoulder and into the water.

"And most impressive move goes to Hayes!" Lawrence clapped his hands as they all laughed at Clint.

Cal sloshed through the creek over to the side and extended his hand to Kara. "I won't throw you. I promise."

She hadn't met Calvin Hastings yet, and her hesitation had all the brothers laughing, knowing full well she had no reason to trust any of them. But Cal had one of those faces, Lawrence presumed, that told women they were safe in his care. And true to his word, he led Kara gently by the hand into the shallowest part of the creek so she could test the water out for herself. Hayes took a couple of steps back and then ran, jumping into the creek with an enormous splash that drenched not only them, but Ruby and Lawrence as well.

Cal laughed as Kara swiped a hand over her face. "Well, I tried."

She grinned and followed him to the middle of the creek where everyone stood or treaded to enjoy the refreshment. Dogs swam or ran along the banks or small stone bridge barking and playing. The sun had started its descent and the evening sunset would be on full display within the next half hour. Lawrence soaked in his surroundings and sighed in pure satisfaction.

"You seem pleased," Ruby stated.

"I am." He looked down at her and to her surprise, ran a gentle hand over her short hair. "I'm just thankful, is all."

Her smile softened as she looked at the others. "Yeah. I know what you mean."

"We're just missing Philip and Helena."

"Oh man, could you imagine Helena being dunked in the water? She'd be worse than Julia." Lawrence laughed at the thought.

"And just like Julia, she'd quickly get over it."

"True enough. She seems to be growing more comfortable with us." He nodded towards Kara.

"Yeah. She is. I'm glad."

He tilted his head as he roamed his gaze over Ruby watching Kara. "You feel like she needs help?"

Ruby looked up at him. "A little. She seems a bit lost, like she's trying to discover who she is again. I want to help her."

He reached over and pulled Ruby into a hug. "You're a good one, Slop. Always have been."

Her arm draped around his waist, as her other hand rested against his chest and her touch had him instantly aware of just how nice she felt in his hold. He cleared his throat and released her, taking a cautious two steps away as he reached into the water beneath his feet and grabbed a clump of mud. "Watch this," he whispered to her, the gleam in his eye only meaning mischief. He tossed the mud at an unassuming Graham, the loud plop that hit him in the side of the head startling everyone.

Julia's hand flew up to cover the laugh that had been her first instinct as Graham swiped fingers over the mud to clear it off his temple. "Well..." His deep voice held a threatening tone and when he looked towards them Lawrence froze.

"Oh no," was Lawrence's last words before Graham slammed into him, tackling him into the water.

H

Chapter Five

Jimmy unlocked the door of his small house behind Sloppy's Diner and motioned for Ruby to step inside. They'd been to the movie theatre in Sheffield, catching the latest movie in some sort of fantasy novel spin-off Jimmy was a fan of. It'd been fun. Ruby enjoyed the movie theatre. She rarely went due to not having time, so it was a nice escape for the evening.

"Looks great in here. I haven't seen it since Cal finished all the updates."

"Oh yeah?" Jimmy flicked on an extra lamp. "It's definitely nicer than what I would have found in Sheffield."

He set his keys on the kitchen counter and walked towards the fridge. "Wine or a beer?"

"Oh, um, water would actually be fine."

"Alright." He fetched a bottle of water and brought it towards her. He hummed with nervous energy as if he wasn't used to having someone in his personal space. Then again, maybe he wasn't. "So, I had fun tonight."

"Me too." She smiled as she took a sip of her water, her eyes bouncing around the cozy house and back to his when she felt him grab her hand. His eyes stared at her lips and she knew he planned to kiss her. His other hand gently cupped her cheek as he leaned in close. Her heart thudded in nervousness. It'd been years since she'd been kissed. *Years.* Just before she was about to close her eyes, she startled and gasped, hopping away from his touch as she pointed over his shoulder. "Snake!"

Jimmy quickly turned around and then relaxed. "Oh. That's Roly."

"Roly? As in your *pet*?" Ruby asked.

"Yeah." He grinned, walking over to the five-foot-long snake, lifting it into his hands, and draping it over his shoulders. He walked towards her and Ruby took a cautious step back as he rested the snakes head in the palm of his hand. "He's a ball python. Don't worry, he's really laid back."

"I-I... you know, I'm just going to take your word for it," Ruby added.

Jimmy smiled as he walked Roly over to the sofa and rested him on the cushions. Ruby promised herself she'd never sit there. A pet snake? Who has a pet *snake?* she shuddered. Her phone buzzed in her pocket, relief filling her as she saw it was Kara at the diner needing help. "Well, that's my summons." She held up the phone. "Kara needs me."

"Oh, alright." Disappointed, Jimmy walked with her to the door. "You want me to walk you over?"

"No, that's okay." She smiled. "I had fun tonight."

"Me too." He gently brushed his thumb over her cheek and pressed a hard kiss to her lips. The force behind the smooch took her by surprise, and she didn't have time to react before he'd pulled away and was waving goodbye. With hurried steps, she walked to the diner, trying to gauge what she'd felt when he'd planted his lips on hers. To her disappointment, she hadn't felt much. And if she were truly honest with herself, she'd admit she didn't like it at all because it just wasn't good. "So disappointing," she whispered, as she opened the back door to the diner and slipped inside to the fragrant kitchen.

Sal reached above his head for the next ticket, while simultaneously sliding two platters on the pickup window and ringing the bell.

"How's it going, Sal?"

"Busy out there. Kara's runnin' her legs off."

"I'll help." Ruby, not dressed in a fancy new dress this time, draped her apron over her jeans and top. She walked through the swinging door and saw Kara's instant relief across the room at the sight of her. She grabbed the two platters, read the table number, and hurried out.

"Here you go." She slid the plates in front of Philip and Clint.

"Hey, Slop," Clint greeted. "Didn't know you were hidin' back there."

"I just got here. You boys chose a busy night."

"Yeah, what's that about?" Philip asked, looking around the crammed diner.

"I don't know. But I like it." Ruby smiled as she hurried back behind the bar to check on the customers that sat on its stools. Kara hurried behind the bar and greeted her with a smile.

"Thanks for coming. It's been swamped since about seven."

"No worries. I'd just gotten back."

"How was your date?" Kara asked.

"I'll fill you in tonight." Ruby crossed her eyes as if there were too much to explain and Kara laughed.

"Sounds good." She grabbed two more plates from the window and rushed them out to a table of awaiting appetites.

To her surprise, Jimmy walked in the front door and made his way to the bar. "Haven't had enough of me, huh?" Ruby teased.

"Well, I figured I'd top off a good night with a good drink."

"The usual?"

"That works." He smiled as she popped the top of his top choice of brew and slid it across the counter. She didn't linger, though, as she hurried to rush a few orders to tables.

A rowdy group of construction workers occupied four tables pulled together in the center of the diner, each with their own feasts and drinks. Sal moved as fast as possible in the kitchen to keep up with their never-ending demand of more food. Kara buzzed by, retrieving empty bottles, replacing them, and replenishing glasses.

Ruby looked up at the sound of the front door opening and Lawrence gave a small wave before surveying the crowded place. He headed straight for his brothers and sat down in a free chair at their table, immediately picking at Philip's fries.

She would fetch his order in a bit, thankful that Lawrence didn't expect her to drop her other customers in favor of him.

"Hey, sweet thang," a voice called from the table of overflowing orange vests. "I need another cold one when you have the chance." Ruby nodded that she heard and hustled behind the bar where Kara stood filling two sodas for the family across the diner. "Have you been keeping tallies on the men at that table?"

Kara pointed to a small paper, the table drawn out with each seat having tallies of how many drinks each customer had purchased. The man in question had only had one, so Ruby marked his second tally down before taking him his fresh drink. He thanked her while another man tugged the corner of her apron with a sly smirk. "Hey sugar, you're the owner of this place, aren't ya?"

"I am," Ruby confirmed.

"You're a little young to run a joint like this, aren't you?"

"Not really." She turned to head back towards the counter, but his grip on her apron remained. "Is there something I can get you?"

"Your number." He winked.

"Sorry, I don't give that out." She tugged her apron from his grasp and hurried towards the Hastings boys. "What will it be, Law?"

"Just a burger. When you have time. No rush."

"I'll let Sal know." She hurried towards the window and slid Lawrence's ticket onto the track for Sal to see.

A few of the patrons at the bar paid their tickets and headed out along with a few tables that'd finished their meals. The crowd was slowly dissipating. Kara's shoulders relaxed a bit as she added money to the tip jar behind the counter. She and Ruby had agreed that all tips would be split 50/50 at the end of each week. Though Ruby missed getting all the money that came in, she also didn't mind the increase in tips since Kara had come on board. The woman was a great waitress and likeable. So, between the two of them, there wasn't too much of a decrease in the amount Ruby usually claimed.

"Am I able to take a breath?" Kara asked.

"Sure. I've got this."

Clint waved his hand from their table.

"I'll go check and see what he needs," Kara offered and hurried towards the table.

With true Hastings charm, Clint had her smiling and laughing before heading back to the bar. "He just needed more ketchup."

"And let me guess, he had a corny joke?"

"Yes. He does have a lot of those, doesn't he?" Kara giggled. "It's fun, though. And a nice reprieve from men like that." She nodded to the construction crew that loudly enjoyed their meal and drinks.

Ruby swiped a towel over the bar top, pausing in front of Jimmy. "You good?" she asked.

"Still sippin'." He held up his bottle as the man who'd claimed ownership over the corner of her apron walked up next to him.

"Hey sugar," he stated again, his comment making her insides crawl. She caught Lawrence's watchful gaze from across the room and was thankful that even in the midst of the chaos, the Hastings brothers were there.

"What can I get you?"

"A pretty little thing like you could get me a lot of things, but I was just wanting a bit of attention." He nudged Jimmy's shoulder as if he should concur with him. "She's playing hard to get."

"I'm sorry, sir, but now is not the time." Ruby hurried away, sweeping platters from the window behind her and carrying Lawrence's burger towards his table. She placed it in front of him while fishing a container of ranch dressing from her apron pocket she knew he'd want.

"That guy bothering you?" Lawrence asked, causing Philip and Clint to glance over towards the bar to see what potential threat stood awaiting her.

"Nothing I can't handle. Enjoy your burger. I'll buzz back by in a bit to see if you need anything."

"Don't bother. If I need something, I'll go to the bar and wait. But I'm fine for now."

She squeezed his shoulder in thanks before jetting off again. She passed Kara and they high-fived as they went their opposite directions. She loved having her around.

Philip and Clint left. Lawrence lingered at the bar talking with Jimmy, and most of the patrons were gone. The construction crew was winding down and standing to head out. Ruby couldn't help the sigh of relief that escaped her when they exited the building. Kara plopped onto a stool. "I just need a minute."

"No worries. Take your time. We have about fifteen minutes before closing."

"I'll take the hint." Lawrence grinned as he tossed some cash on the bar.

"You already paid, Law," Ruby reminded him.

"Consider it a tip."

Kara's eyes widened at the amount and Ruby rolled her eyes as she scooped it up and stuffed it into the tip jar beneath the counter. "Be careful heading home."

"I will." He shook Jimmy's hand before donning his cowboy hat. "You ladies have a good night." He tipped his head towards Kara before waltzing his lazy, long-legged stride to the exit. She and Kara both watched him leave. He was the type of man you wanted to watch. Strong back, long legs, and just enough swagger to catch any woman's eye.

"One of those 'I hate to see him go, but love to watch him leave' moments," Kara whispered and had Ruby stifling a giggle, knowing full well her new friend was right. Lawrence, along with the other Hastings brothers, was easy on the eyes. And she'd be lying if she hadn't thought about him a couple of times since seeing him bathing her dog in the creek. She wasn't sure she could ever scrub that memory from her mind.

A throat cleared behind them and Ruby's eyes rounded as she realized Jimmy still sat at the bar witnessing their gawking after Lawrence. She turned and offered an upbeat smile as if she weren't just drooling over her friend. "You good to get home? Do I need to call you a cab?" she teased.

"I think I can manage." He smiled. "Thanks again for this evening, Ruby. I had fun." He leaned towards her and brushed his lips over her cheek, hesitating a moment to see if she potentially wanted more than that. She didn't move. Not that she wasn't thinking about kissing him. She was. It was just that Kara stood a few feet away watching their interaction and... well, Ruby still hadn't gotten over the first initial kiss he planted on her. She didn't really want another bad kiss. Feeling guilty for that thought, she walked with him to the door and locked it behind him.

"That bad, huh?" Kara asked.

"It's so disappointing."

Kara's sympathetic smile had Ruby confessing her disappointment and lack of thrill at his earlier lip lock which took them the rest of clean-up to discuss and the walk to Ruby's house to dissect. When she'd showered, crawled into her bed, and turned off the lamp, Kara taking temporary residence in her guest room, Ruby relaxed and realized that perhaps one more kiss would help better determine if Jimmy was worth pursuing. She'd been distracted by his snake. *Snake.* She cringed. Perhaps a fresh chance and opportunity was what they needed to test the chemistry level between them. She added 'Kiss Jimmy' to her to-do list. He was too nice not to give it another shot.

They needed rain. What little they'd received, several weeks prior had greened up the place for a few brief days, but the summer sun did its job and burned everything back down to a crisp. The roads were in need of repair, but without rain to tamper down the dust, there was no point in even starting that project. So, despite his disappointment of not driving the maintainer over ranch roads, Calvin lowered his welding helmet and helped Lawrence with repairs to the cow pens. They were on their last side of the pens for repairs, then they'd rescue Clint from Graham's bossing and setting of new posts by beginning the work of welding the two new pen extensions. He'd have a couple of weeks invested in this project, but it would be worth it come spring when they work cows. He was also grateful for Cal's help, knowing his brother would not only rather smooth roads, but also clear brush. Instead, Seth worked his way along the fence line in a skid steer in a neighboring acreage to get a head start on clearing.

Hayes, training three new horses, had his hands full at the stables. And Philip, usually up at the feed store, was helping cut pipe a few feet away and lining them up according to Graham's pen drafts. It was hot work, late summer always bringing some of the hottest temperatures for the year, but Lawrence soaked it up. He loved working with his hands. He loved having projects, and he loved seeing his hard work and sweat come to fruition. Dolly panted in the shade beneath his truck as she watched him work. He loved having her companionship on the job these days. Cal's dog, Hobbs, rested beside her, completely asleep as the sounds of metal and spark failed to phase him.

"So anyway, Helena said her dad and brother would love to come out if given the opportunity." Clint explained to Graham, still pitching his hunting enterprise idea.

"If we can line them up for this fall, it will give us practice on what to expect for next year."

"I thought you were leavin' in October?" Graham asked.

"I am," Clint confirmed. "I'll be guiding on a ranch in New Mexico until January. But Seth has agreed to guide them this round. They'd stay in my house, which would be made spotless by the wonderful Annie, who has also agreed to play cook for that weekend. They'd receive the royal treatment while here.

"And how much is this going to cost?" Graham asked, always focused on the numbers.

"For us, just a few bags of corn. Time. I've got game cameras ready to go. Will start putting them up towards the end of this month, starting in the acreage behind my place because that's where you said you saw the biggest bucks, though you're terrible at scoring them. So I'll be guessing the first few weeks on camera placement. But I've got time. So once the weather turns, we'll see if the deer start movin', but I have a feeling they'll keep to the feeders over there to start."

Graham didn't say a word as he slammed the fence pole driver on top of the metal pipe and drove it into the ground. Clint, surprisingly, waited patiently for his brother to sort through all the information he'd just dumped on him.

"Let me look at the numbers again tonight. If I give you a set amount I'm willing to invest in this, you can stick with it?"

"Yes sir." Clint's excitement was on the edge of bubbling over, but he kept his cool.

"Alright. I'll look over your plans tonight and at the budget."

"Thanks, Graham."

Clint walked towards the trailer to retrieve some more pipe and shot a discreet thumbs up towards Lawrence on his way.

"Yoo hoo!" Annie's voice called out as she made her way towards them. "You boys are out here in the heat of the day doin' this?" She tsked her tongue at Graham.

"It's got to get done, Annie," he replied.

"But not at two o clock in the afternoon on one of the hottest days in August. Look at poor Cal's face." She nodded towards his brother, who'd lifted his welding helmet to wipe sweat from his eyes, his face beet-red and dripping. "That water cooler full?" She pointed to the bed of Graham's truck and he nodded. "Good." She rested her hands on her hips as the men continued working.

Lawrence looked up, lifting his helmet. "What brings you out, Annie?"

"I wanted a word with you."

"Me?" he asked curiously.

"Yes, you, Lawrence."

He removed his helmet and brushed his sleeve over his damp face as he walked towards her.

"What is it? Henry okay? I promise I didn't mean to cause a war between you two when I bought him that handheld Jeopardy game."

She smirked. "No. That's not why I'm here, though I'm not sure I have forgiven you for that yet. Come to the car with me." She walked towards her vehicle, the engine still running and air conditioner blasting. "I wanted to talk to you a minute because I'm concerned. And I know you of all people would know more about it than anyone else."

"Alright..." He waited, completely clueless as to what Annie could possibly think he knew.

"Ruby."

"What about her?"

"Is she okay?" Annie asked.

"Why wouldn't she be?"

"Well, she's been dating Jimmy, and I just don't know about him, Lawrence."

"Why? What's wrong with him?"

"Nothing's wrong with him," she amended.

"Okay..."

She sighed, her worried expression causing him to rest a hand on her shoulder. "Tell me what's got you bothered."

"I just don't know about him, that's all. I like the boy, I do. But there's just something off about him. When I see them together, Ruby doesn't look... smitten. And well, I'm worried she's putting too much effort into that boy and he's wasting her time."

"Ah. And you think I'd know more about this?"

"Well, yes. You and Ruby have always been close. I was just wondering if she'd mentioned anything to you, you know, about how she feels about him."

"Sounds like you don't want her to get serious with him."

"I don't," Annie replied. "At first, I was excited for her. But when he took her to Bargain Burger—" She shook her head in complete irritation. "What man does that when he has such a pretty thing to flaunt?"

Lawrence chuckled.

"And then they went to a movie the other night in Sheffield, and Ruby said it was fine. Just *fine*."

"Okay…"

"*Fine*, Lawrence," she reiterated. "Just fine. A date should be more than just fine, especially if you're interested in someone."

"Annie…" He contemplated what to say. Annie wouldn't have driven out to the ranch and sought him out if she wasn't truly concerned. He hadn't talked to Ruby about Jimmy really, which, he had to admit, was odd, considering they usually did talk about everything together. But just because they hadn't didn't mean something was wrong with the guy or Ruby's feelings towards him. He liked Jimmy well enough. He was a bit on the delicate side, Lawrence thought, but that came from working inside all day, and that could also just be him wanting to find a flaw in the guy because he was interested in Ruby. They all felt protective of her. She was theirs. Always had been.

So for a man to come into the picture and begin to direct her attention elsewhere, it was a bit unsettling for all of them. Especially if they weren't sure of the man's intentions towards her.

"You want me to have a talk with Ruby or Jimmy?" Lawrence asked.

"Both," Annie told him. "I want to know where they're both at on this. Just put the feelers out for me. I just don't have a settled spirit over it." She tapped her heart. "And you know I've got the gift. I knew the moment I met Julia she would be with Graham. And I knew Helena would capture Philip's heart. And we all knew Alice and Calvin were destined for one another ever since she shoved him in the mud when they were two. And as much as I like Jimmy, the boy just doesn't fit with our Ruby," she fretted.

"I'll talk to them. Somehow," Lawrence offered.

"Thank you, Sweetie. You know how I worry about all of you." She hugged him, not caring about his sweaty shirt clinging to his skin. "And don't make it sound like I'm being nosy. I'm not."

He smiled at her. "You're always nosy, Annie."

She gasped in offense. "I am not. I'm concerned, worried, investigative, and loving."

He laughed. "Investigative. Nice one."

She playfully swatted him. "Posh. Get back to work. Thank you for listening to my concerns, Lawrence. You'd tell me if you had concerns too, right?"

"Yes."

"And you don't have any?"

"No."

He could tell that made her feel better.

"Alright. Maybe this feeling is nothing and I'm overreacting. But I just needed to check it out. I'll have peace about it once you talk with her. You'll let me know?"

"I'll go up to Sloppy's tonight and have dinner."

"You're an angel, Lawrence Dean. Come by the house afterwards and I'll reward you with dessert."

"Yes ma'am." He tipped his head towards her as she climbed back into her car and drove away.

Cal walked up with Graham and Clint. "What was that about?" he asked.

"She's worried about Ruby."

"Something wrong?" Graham asked.

"Just doesn't know what to think of Jimmy, is all."

"And she drove out here to talk to you about it?" Clint asked. "Wow, she must really not like him."

"I don't think it's that," Lawrence acknowledged. "I think it's because it's Ruby and she's nervous he's not the right match for her."

"Can't anyone just casually date?" Clint asked. "It's not like every person you date has to be your match. Jimmy's a good guy. Even if he's not the one Slop falls in love with, at least she's able to have a little fun outside of that diner."

"I agree. But Annie's protective of Ruby."

"We all are," Graham reminded him, still concerned that Annie had driven all the way to the ranch to voice her worries.

"I'm going up there for supper tonight to talk with Ruby and possibly Jimmy. Subtly. To see if I can put Annie's mind at ease."

"Want us to go with?" Graham asked.

"I don't want to scare them, Graham." Lawrence laughed as he slapped his brother's arm in good fun.

"Right. Well, leave a little early so you can talk with her before the dinner rush," Graham ordered.

Lawrence nodded and walked back to his work, Cal hot on his heels.

"So weird," Cal muttered.

"Yeah."

"You think there's something about Jimmy we're all missing?"

"No."

"But Annie doesn't get all riled up about nothing," Calvin pointed out.

"No, but again, she's protective of Ruby. She'd be like this over anyone. Even if it were you or me."

"You think so?"

"Yes." Lawrence lifted his helmet from the ground. "Now are we going to get more work done or do I need to brew some tea?"

Lowering his helmet, Calvin pointed to the pipe they'd been working on and sparked the torch.

H

Chapter Six

"*I have time to* chat for a bit." Ruby motioned towards a small table of the construction workers from a few nights prior that'd come in after their day's work and had settled into their meals with as much enthusiasm as they had the last time. Kara had the night off and Ruby and Sal manned the diner alone. "What's up?"

"Not much." Lawrence sat at the bar, having arrived right at five to give him some time with Ruby before the supper patrons started filtering in. "Just hadn't talked to you in a while. How are things?"

"Pretty good." She shrugged her shoulders. "Can't complain."

"Things workin' out with Kara pretty well?"

"She's amazing. I'm so thankful I brought her on board. I honestly don't know how I did it without her."

"Good." Lawrence took a sip of his tea, the condensation on his glass showing he'd wasted enough time with small talk and needed to get to the point. "And things with Jimmy? How's that going?"

Ruby sighed, leaning forward on the bar top as she stole one of his chips and popped it into her mouth. "It's okay."

"Just okay?"

Her shoulders lifted and dropped again. "It's nice to have someone to do things with."

"But that's all it is?"

"I don't know. I'm still trying to figure that out."

Easy enough, he thought.

"Well, he seems like a nice guy. Seems to like you."

"He does, I think." She smiled and then it disappeared.

"What? What is it?" Lawrence's protective nerves tingled.

"Can I bounce something off of you?"

"Of course. You know you can." He motioned for her to continue.

"Have you ever liked someone, like a lot, and then when you see their personal side, there's just some oddities that just weird you out?"

His brows rose. "Now I'm intrigued."

She laughed. "I'm serious, Law."

"I guess it depends on the oddity. Are we talking like an extra toe? A collection of pygmy pig figurines? What?"

She giggled into her hand and shook her head. "No. Stop it."

He grinned.

"Well... okay, so I'm just going to tell you what happened."

"Shoot," he encouraged.

"So, we went to the movies and then went back to his place."

Lawrence's gut twisted, he wasn't liking the sound of this already.

"And he was going to kiss me, right? Which, I kind of wanted, you know, to see if our chemistry was … well, you know." She blushed. "Any way, as he was about to kiss me this giant snake appears behind him."

"A snake?" Lawrence's brows shot up.

"A *snake*," Ruby confirmed. "A ball python to be exact. His *pet*."

"Who in the h— I mean, who in the world has a snake for a pet?"

"Exactly!" She shimmied her shoulders. "It totally freaked me out!"

Lawrence laughed and she tossed a chip at him. He held up his hand. "I'm sorry, I'm sorry. So what happened?"

"Well, I hightailed it out of there." Ruby pointed to the bar. "Thankfully, Kara had texted me for help, so it gave me a good excuse."

"Poor Jimmy. You don't like his snake and he didn't get to kiss you."

"Oh, he kissed me," she added, Lawrence's tea souring in his mouth at that thought.

"Oh?"

"And it was… *not* good." She covered her face with her hands.

His lips twitched.

"Please don't laugh, I'm seriously so confused."

"Not going to laugh," he promised, though his face struggled to maintain its seriousness. Her doubtful expression had him grinning. "Okay, so how was it bad?"

"It was just too... quick," She replied. "And maybe that was because I was in a hurry to leave after seeing Roly. Yeah, that's his snake's name. Roly. And he sort of just planted one on me. I wasn't even ready. I didn't even really have a moment to take it in. It was a quick, forceful press of the lips and then I was facing the doorway."

Lawrence grimaced.

"Yeah, so not romantic. And I haven't really been able to figure out if I should pursue him any further because I felt nothing."

"I think it's too quick to rule him out. It was just one kiss. Give the guy time to plant one on you for real."

"True, it was rushed. But the snake?"

"Look, maybe he's just fostering it until he finds a zoo or something."

"A zoo? Really?" She narrowed her eyes at him and he chuckled.

"I don't know. Maybe that's not a deal breaker.

"Would you have a snake?"

"Heck no." Lawrence shook his head. "The only good snake is a dead snake, in my opinion."

"I feel the same. And if I told him I didn't like his snake, I think it would hurt his feelings. I mean, I'd be sad if he didn't like Porter."

"Um, Porter is awesome," Lawrence defended the pup and she smiled. "He's just young and needs more training."

"But still, I'd be insulting his beloved pet if I told him it freaked me out."

"I see the dilemma."

"Anyways, you asked, and I know you probably weren't wanting that much info, but there ya go. That's where I'm at with that."

"Hey, it's my duty to check in on you every now and then. And I don't mind hearing you out." Lawrence tapped his glass. "Can you top me off?"

She grabbed it and walked it to the tea decanter and began filling his glass. The door to the diner opened and Jimmy, still dressed in his vet clothes, walked inside. He smiled in greeting, Ruby casting Lawrence a hard gaze to keep his mouth shut about what they'd just discussed. "Hi," she greeted, sliding Lawrence his cup. "You're here early."

"Finished up early with the help of Julia. Alice was out on calls all day, so Julia and I ran the clinic. She cleans like a madwoman all day so she can buzz out right at five to get home to see Graham. Makes for an earlier evening for me, so I'm not complaining." He shook Lawrence's hand. "How's it going?"

"Good. Just buggin' Slop here."

A whistle sounded from the table of men behind them and Ruby glanced up and sighed. "Be right back."

"Did they seriously just whistle at her?" Lawrence asked.

"Yep. They've been here every evening since working on the highway north of town. They're something else."

Ruby hurried into the kitchen and walked out carrying a fresh batch of onion rings towards the men. She placed it on the table and listened as several of them spoke over one another. "Where's that stripper girl of yours?"

"Excuse me?" Ruby's back stiffened.

"You know, the pretty one from Sheffield? She workin' over there tonight?"

Lawrence turned at the conversation and Jimmy swiveled around as well.

Ruby planted both hands on her hips.

"Uh oh," Lawrence muttered. "She's about to let them have it."

"Now, you listen here," She pointed a finger in the man's face, her harsh tone and fierce stance surprising all the men at the table. "My waitress is a wonderful woman. She's beautiful, smart, and kind. She's working here so she doesn't have to work there and have the likes of you drooling all over her. And if you think you can storm into this diner and treat her with disrespect, or even whisper about her life or work, you can take your business elsewhere. I will not have you bullying, harassing, or gawking at my waitress or anyone else who steps foot in here. Is that understood?"

The man smirked. "Sure thing, sugar. I was just curious is all."

"Well, curiosity killed the cat," Ruby retorted.

"And satisfaction brought him back," the man countered.

"Until I shot him with a shotgun," Ruby finished and stormed back towards the bar. Her last parting words silenced the man for a few minutes before he was back to chumming it up with his friends.

"The nerve," she ranted quietly. "And this is why Kara tiptoes around people. She's trying so hard to start fresh and people like that just strip her of all dignity."

"You did good, Slop," Lawrence told her.

"Well, I'm just thankful Kara isn't here tonight. I would have hated for her to hear that. She's made so much progress in shedding her shame, that would have set her back months. Pig," she mumbled again, still struggling with keeping her temper.

"Hey, sugar!" the man called again.

"Are you kidding me?" Ruby forced a smile on her face. "Be right back."

She walked back towards the table.

Lawrence and Jimmy turned to make sure the man behaved. He saw the shock cross Ruby's face at whatever the man said and the faint pink flush climbing up her neck. He knew that only meant one thing, the man had overstepped. Big time. "He just said something to insult her."

"How do you know?" Jimmy asked.

"She's shutting down." Lawrence saw Ruby's shoulders slowly start to sag and her hands twitched in nerves as she fumbled her towel in her hands.

She hurried back behind the bar in quick steps.

"What did he say to you?"

She shook her head, her eyes starting to mist over. "Slop?" Lawrence tapped the counter.

"It was nothing," she hissed through her teeth. "They're about to leave."

Lawrence began to stand, and she placed a restraining hand on his. "Don't. Just let it go."

"I want to know what happened," he demanded, Jimmy watching Ruby's face as if he wasn't quite sure how to respond.

"He was just... bold. That's all."

"Did he—"

"Lawrence, stop," she barked. "Just let it be." She hurried over to the register and typed up their ticket and hurried it over to the table, careful to avoid the end the man sat on, though his eyes followed her like a hawk.

"I don't like it." Lawrence looked to Jimmy. "You going to be around a while."

"Yep."

"Good. Because when I leave, I want someone here."

"I'll be here until about eight or so."

"Good." He watched as the men stood and left, Ruby's demeanor relieved.

Lawrence waited for her to buzz back by the bar. "You not eating?" she asked him.

"No. I'm going to bug Philip for a bit. He worked out at the ranch today, so naturally I have to prolong his agony and impose on him at home." He grinned. "You good?"

"I'm fine," she assured him. "They're gone, so I'm fine."

"Alright." Lawrence looked to Jimmy. "Keep an eye on her."

Ruby rolled her eyes. "I'm fine, Lawrence. Go."

Hesitant, but knowing he was going to stay in town until the diner closed so as to walk her home, Lawrence left and headed towards Philip's house.

∞

Most nights Ruby had to make herself quit and leave the diner. She'd always find one more thing to do if she stayed long enough. But some nights, like tonight, she enjoyed flipping the sign on the door and locking up. She would enjoy her walk home. It allowed her to breathe the fresh air and decompress after a long day. And though the construction crew had left hours ago, she still felt the creepy crawlies on her skin from the man and his offer of inappropriate advances towards her during his meal.

Jimmy stood beside her as she locked up. "Well, that's that." She looked up at him. "Thanks for staying later. You didn't have to."

He shrugged. "It was no problem. I'm happy if it gave you a little peace of mind."

"It did." She smiled as he walked towards the edge of the slanted porch to head around the back towards his house. As he rounded the corner, her smile faded at the sound of a truck door closing and the horrible man from earlier stepped out of his truck with a smirk. "Need a ride home, sugar?"

"No. Thank you." Ruby wished Porter were waiting for her on the porch with Roughneck Randy, but she'd left the dog at home so he didn't have to suffer from the heat of the day. She glanced towards the edge of the porch and felt like Jimmy shouldn't be too far and she could probably catch up to him. "Jimmy!" she called. "Wait up!" She tried to sound nonchalant as she offered a quick wave to the creepy man and headed towards the edge of the porch. The man stood in the center of the parking lot, his hands in his pockets and in no hurry to leave.

Jimmy poked his head around the corner of the building. "Everything okay?"

She tilted her head to the man and Jimmy stiffened. "Have a good night, sir. I've got it from here." He offered a friendly wave to the man as he draped his arm over Ruby's shoulders as if he were leading her home.

"Thank you," she whispered.

"No problem."

"Now, I just needed a word with her," the man continued, taking a few steps in their direction.

Jimmy turned, uncertainty on his face. Ruby's heart tripped and she felt her hands slowly start to shake as the man continued to progress his way towards them. There would be a fight, of that she had no doubt. And she prayed nothing bad would happen to Jimmy or herself. She prayed the man would trip or lose interest as the hour grew later, but he kept walking towards them. Jimmy's arm went slack and slipped off her shoulders, stealing what little security she'd felt.

"I don't think he's leaving," Jimmy whispered.

"What do we do?"

"Let's just... keep calm and hear him out. Maybe he'll get bored and leave."

She didn't like the plan but didn't feel like they had much of a choice.

"You mind giving us a minute?" the man asked Jimmy.

Jimmy hesitated and then took a few steps away, Ruby inwardly panicking that he'd now separated from her.

"Now, sugar, I know I came off as a bit crude earlier."

"A bit?" Ruby gawked. "You're kidding right? You were disgusting and rude." She could tell her comment irritated him.

"Now, let's not act out. I might have t—"

"Have to what?" a deep voice asked from behind her. Relief swept through her at the sound of Lawrence's voice. "I suggest you get in your truck and leave."

"Oh now, you can't tell me to do that." The man's voice dropped to a sinister tone.

"I can and I did. Leave."

The man took a step towards Ruby and Lawrence grabbed her arm and slung her behind him, intercepting the man in the middle. Fury ignited behind the man's eyes.

"You think you can stop me? That little lady's been askin' for trouble from the moment she spotted me. And then earlier, gettin' sassy with me and playin' hard to get... she thrives on this. Can't you tell?"

"I think you're misreading this situation," Lawrence warned. "I don't want to hear anything you have to say. This is not two bros discussing their options. This is me telling you to leave or I will *make* you leave."

The man stepped forward and Lawrence sighed in disappointment. "Really?" He held his hands out to his sides.

"Law, just... let's go," Ruby said, her voice slightly quivering. Jimmy stood to the side still, his face showing complete bewilderment at what was about to transpire.

Grinning, the man swatted a hand out, tapping Lawrence's hat off his head and sending it to the dirt. A bullet could never be as quick as Lawrence Hastings in that moment. He grabbed the front of the man's shirt and lifted him several inches off the ground before tossing him into the dirt. Rage radiated off of Lawrence's back as he stalked towards the man, the creep finally understanding he'd messed with the wrong person. He scrambled to his feet and braced himself for Lawrence's punch, though Lawrence's fists never left his side. "You have two seconds."

Terrified of Lawrence's strength, the man hurried to his truck and peeled out of the parking lot, gravel spitting behind him. Lawrence stood and watched until the taillights disappeared up the road.

Ruby placed a cautious hand on his arm and he instantly softened, though she could still feel adrenaline pumping through him. "Thank you," she whispered, her words barely a whisper as a tear slipped down her cheek.

Lawrence tugged her into a tight hug, his eyes connecting with Jimmy's over the top of her head. Without a word, the vet tech silently retreated towards his house.

H

Chapter Seven

"*And you didn't kill* him?" Alice asked, tossing a roll of medical tape at Lawrence as she wrapped Hayes's split elbow in a bandage.

"No. I didn't have to. He got the hint." Lawrence shoveled another load of horse manure and tossed it into the wheelbarrow. He didn't enjoy mucking stalls, but Hayes, having been bucked off one of the horses he'd been training, had landed wrong on his elbow and split the skin. He needed help while Alice stitched him back together, and Lawrence had enough rage from the night before still pulsing through his system that he needed some physical labor to vent it out on.

"Can't believe that happened to Slop." Hayes shook his head in remorse. "How's she holdin' up?"

Good, I guess. She's up at the main house with Julia. Left her there a while ago."

"Julia will cluck over her." Alice nodded in approval at his decision.

"She didn't sleep a wink last night. Well, maybe for like five minutes and then I could hear her cry a bit more." Lawrence spit into the hay, disgusted not only with the dust in his mouth, but the thought of Ruby crying. "I don't know what that man offered, implied, or said, but it got under her skin and terrified her."

"I'm glad you brought her to the ranch," Alice said. "She can always stay with us if need be."

"I didn't want to wake y'all up. She slept in my room."

Hayes and Alice both popped their eyes up at him at that statement.

He growled. "Not with me." He tossed the dung into the wheelbarrow. "I slept on the couch. Seth was already asleep in his room, so I let her have mine. I was trying to be a gentleman."

"And you were," Alice assured him. "You took care of her. That's what family does."

"Porter knew something was up to when we picked him up from her house. He stuck to her like glue. Dolly, too, once she stepped into the house."

"We'll keep her here for a couple days. At least over the weekend." Alice snipped the tape and gently rotated Hayes's arm. "How does that feel?"

"Better. Thanks."

"No problem. You boys keep me in business." Alice looked to Lawrence. "You told Annie what happened yet?"

"No."

Hayes whistled under his breath.

"It's not my news to tell."

"Lawrence—" Alice touched his arm and then immediately withdrew her hand at the spark of anger in his gaze. "I'll call her."

"The last thing Ruby wants is for everyone to feel sorry for her. She had a bad night. We handled it. The more people that try and coddle her, the more she's going to get quiet and angry."

"Alright, fine. I won't say anything to Annie. I'll offer her our couch and a girls' night tonight. Unless she has plans with Jimmy."

"She doesn't. Or she won't. At least not after I'm through with him," Lawrence added.

"What happened with Jimmy?"

"Nothing. That's the problem," Lawrence railed on. "He just stood there like Adam, passive and noncommitted. That man was tryin' to grab her, and Jimmy just stepped back and offered her up. I don't care how much he likes her, he's not gettin' near her unless it's as friends."

"Isn't that Ruby's call?" Hayes asked.

"No." Lawrence huffed. "Fine, yes. It is. But she'd be smart not to pursue that guy anymore. His backbone is still in the diner parking lot if you go looking for it."

Alice bit back a smirk. "I'm going to head back to the house. Finish venting before you come back."

"I'm not ventin'." Lawrence tossed the shovel against the wall and grabbed the handles of the wheelbarrow and barreled through the barn to dump it out back.

"Thoughts?" Alice asked Hayes.

"I'd say Jimmy and the creepy guy should be thankful they have any skin left, much less their lives."

"Poor Slop," Alice sighed. "She definitely deserves better."

"Well, maybe now she'll get it." Hayes nodded in Lawrence's direction as he parked the wheelbarrow and began bringing in loads of fresh hay.

"Possibly." Alice patted Hayes on the back. "See you two later."

"Thanks again, Al. I appreciate the mending."

"Anytime. Work his anger out until he's tame, Hayes."

Chuckling, Hayes nodded. "I'll do my best. Go see about Sloppy."

Lawrence saw Alice retreat to her truck and head back in the direction of Graham's house. Thankful for peace, he groaned when Hayes walked up with a winning smile and an eagerness to help.

"Just let me work, Hayes."

"I don't think you need to. I see your steam wearing off. I think it's time you go cool down instead." He pointed towards the creek. "Go. Fish. Do something relaxing. You're a hero who's come home from war. And won."

"Give me a break." Lawrence couldn't help but smirk at Hayes's description.

"Alright, maybe that's too glamorous. How about you catch some fish and I'll fry 'em up later?"

"Now, that I think I can do. Thanks." Lawrence accepted the pat on his back on the way out of the barn and into the sunshine. A lazy day of fishing would do him good, because Lord knew he needed to relax after last night.

∞

Alice plopped down onto Graham's sofa, the oldest brother looking up from the agriculture magazine he read in his chair. "Alice," he greeted before putting his nose back in the pages.

"Hey, old man."

Not dignifying her comment with a response, Graham asked, "You get Hayes taken care of?"

"Don't I always?"

He silently turned a page as Julia and Ruby walked into the living room.

"How is he?" Ruby asked.

"Fine. Just a few stitches."

"Not Hayes." Ruby waved away Alice's response. "I mean, not that he isn't important... or his welfare... but I meant Lawrence."

"He's fuming still. And worried about you. Did you expect anything less?"

Ruby's hands twisted in her lap as she sat in the far corner of the deep leather sofa. She ignored Graham's silent but strong presence as she fretted. "I thought he might be."

"Give him a few hours. He'll tone down."

"Yeah…" Ruby's eyes fell to her lap.

"You have nothing to be ashamed of, Ruby," Julia said. "Sometimes the only thing a man will listen to is another man. Lawrence defending you was the right thing to do in that situation. You didn't cause that man's horrid behavior."

"As Annie would say, that's a heart issue. There's something not right there if he's treating women like he is," Alice chimed in.

"I know. It's just frustrating that Law had to step in. I can typically handle those types of patrons. Trust me, this isn't the first time a nasty man has given me a hard time over the years. But this guy…" She shivered at the thought of him coming near her. "He scared me. I'm grateful Lawrence turned up when he did. The night could have ended a lot differently."

The silent turn of a magazine page had the women glancing Graham's direction. Julia cleared her throat and he lowered it just enough to peer over the top. She widened her eyes and then darted her glance to the door. He took the hint and cleared his throat, setting his magazine aside. "I need to check on the stables," he mumbled, rising to his feet and quickly making himself scarce.

Ruby smiled tenderly at his departing back, grateful for his thoughtfulness and acknowledgement of her need of women time.

"And Jimmy? Have you checked with him this morning?" Julia asked.

Ruby shook her head. "I texted him, but he hasn't responded yet. He probably won't."

"Why?" Alice asked. "It's not like you did anything wrong."

Ruby shrugged.

Calvin walked up the porch steps, his boots scraping against the edges causing the women to peek out the screen door. "Don't come in here, Cal," Alice called. "You're filthy and Julia mopped yesterday."

Cal removed his cowboy hat and regrettably looked at the manure and dirt he'd scraped on Graham's front steps.

"Don't worry about it, Cal." Julia grinned.

"I'm lookin' for Lawrence."

"He was at the stables," Al told him.

"Got it." Knowing all the brothers knew of her debacle, but being sweet not to make her feel any more uncomfortable than she already felt, Ruby met his understanding gaze and gave him a nod that she was fine. Calvin took the silent cue and retreated back down the front steps and to his truck.

"I love that man." Alice shook her head. "And I could stare after him all... day... long."

Ruby placed her cold cup on Alice's leg, causing her friend to jump in place. "I think you need to cool down." Ruby fanned her with a smile. She glanced down as her cell phone rang. "It's Kara." She answered and then placed a hand to her forehead. "I'm so sorry, Kara. I forgot to call you and tell you I've closed the diner down for the weekend. Wow, I am so sorry." She listened a moment. "I'm at the ranch right now and plan to stay for a bit, why don't you come out here? Remember how to get here?" She paused and listened again. "Alright, see you in a bit." She ended the call. "Well, I feel terrible. I forgot to tell Kara she didn't need to come in today and she's driven in from Sheffield. She's headed this way." Ruby relaxed against the cushions before sitting upright again. "Oh, and please don't tell her what that man said about her at the diner."

"We wouldn't," Julia assured her. "She's sweet and I can tell she's truly wanting to put her past behind her, so it would serve absolutely no purpose to mention it."

"Agreed," Alice added.

"Thanks."

"So... are we going to talk about the elephant in the room?" Alice wriggled her eyebrows.

"What elephant?" Ruby and Julia asked.

"Come on, Jewels, you of all people should have picked up on it."

"What?" Genuinely perplexed, Julia slid her legs underneath her as she sank deeper into Graham's recliner.

"The fact Lawrence was able to pick up a grown man and toss him like a hay sprig." Alice danced her fingers up Ruby's arm. "Isn't that how you described it?"

Ruby laughed. "I admit, I was impressed. The man's shoes literally lifted a few inches off the ground, and he wasn't little."

Julia grinned. "Are we really that surprised?"

"Oh, did you know Lawrence was packin' those kind of guns?" Alice asked.

"You two were at the creek the other day, right? I mean, he wasn't exactly covering up his physique," Julia added. "I was surprised he was so... muscley."

Ruby covered her mouth and giggled as Alice hooted. "Look out, Graham."

Julia waved her comment away. "Please. As impressive as Lawrence was, nothing can compare to Graham."

"Oh? And have you seen him shirtless? When? You haven't told me. Do tell," Alice continued baiting, making her friend blush.

"Stop it." Julia laughed. "And yes, I have seen him shirtless because I helped him remove blood stains from his shirt the other day from when Seth was knocked in the shin by a calf. Graham helped him out and stained his shirt in the process."

"So you helped him take it off so you could 'wash' it?" Alice continued.

Julia tossed a throw pillow at her as Ruby laughed, thankful for girl talk and good friends.

"I'm just sayin', I didn't know Lawrence had it in him."

"Well, when adrenaline pumps through your veins you can take on challenges you normally wouldn't," Julia added.

"I'm thankful he did it, adrenaline or no adrenaline. Jimmy just stood there."

Alice waved Jimmy's name out of the air like a bothersome fly. "He lost my vote when you said he was a bad kisser."

"I didn't say he was bad." Ruby held her head in her hands a moment. "Just that that particular kiss was bad."

"Still." Alice shrugged as if it didn't matter. "Tomato, to-mah-to. I like him, don't get me wrong, but if he can't stand up for his girl, even if it means he'll get pummeled, then he doesn't have my vote."

"Especially when a hunky cowboy steps in, full of swagger and charm, lifting a man feet off the ground," Julia exaggerated, her fist slowly rising into the air like she was about to burst into song or lead a rally. "And tossing him aside like a rotten to-mah-to."

Alice returned the throw pillow in Julia's direction as she laughed.

"Knock knock," Helena's east Texas drawl called from behind the screen door.

"Helena!" Julia gushed. "I didn't know you were going to be in Parks this weekend." She opened the door and waved her in.

"Acting like this is already her house," Alice whispered to Ruby.

"It suits her."

"Oh yeah," Alice agreed and silenced as the other two women came into the living room.

"We're just chattin' girl talk. Muscles, handsome men, and how Ruby should fall in love with Lawrence." Alice's last remark had Ruby's eyes bulging.

"Wait— We are not talking about that last one."

Helena perched on the edge of a chair. "Well, I'm glad I got here in time. Sounds juicy."

"Where's Phil?" Julia asked.

"Oh, he was headed to help Lawrence with the cow pens."

"Lawrence isn't working on the pens." Alice stalked over towards the porch and stepped outside. "I'll be darned, he is. That boy." She shook her head. "Hayes was supposed to help him relax."

"He's a Hastings," Ruby said. "Isn't work *how* they relax?"

"True."

"So, Helena, question," Alice stated.

"Okay." Helena tucked her hair behind her ear.

"Is Philip a good kisser?"

Helena's slow smile answered the question before she did.

"And Jewels, is Graham a good kisser?"

"Oh. Yeah." She fanned herself as the women laughed.

"And Cal is a good kisser, so the odds are that Lawrence is a good kisser too, Slop. Go for it."

"Why do you want to hook me up with Lawrence so bad? We're friends. He defended me. I didn't swoon and fall in love just because he stood up for me. If that were the case, I'd have fallen in love with him a long time ago, because half his life he's defended me against bullies. Do you not remember my childhood? I was teased relentlessly unless Lawrence stepped in. This is nothing new."

Alice quietly took a sip of her water. "Just saying he's a decent option."

"I agree. But not for me," Ruby reiterated. "He hasn't even spoken to me this morning. That's how *not* big of a deal it was to him."

"I disagree," Alice said. "He was pretty fired up about it this morning at the stables."

Ruby stood. "Fine. I'll go talk to him now. You'll see he's totally fine and we're fine as friends."

"Okay." Alice waved her out the door and then turned to the other two. "It's so going to happen."

Julia and Helena both nodded in agreement as they all walked towards the front door to move their party to the front porch.

H

Chapter Eight

"So why add onto the pens?" Kara asked, turning as Ruby approached.

"It provides a low stress weaning area for the cows and calves. They can be near their mommas but not be in the same pen."

"Could you not just put them in another pasture?" she asked curiously.

Lawrence, always pleased to talk ranch work, nodded at her consideration. "Some ranchers do that," he began. "but by doing it this way, they take to the feed faster. We set feed troughs along here." He motioned up what would be fence line. "Water troughs in the middle. They are healthier being closer to their mommas."

"I see."

He looked up at Ruby's approach. "I'm educating her on all things cows."

"Lucky her." Ruby smiled. "No better teacher."

"I'd argue that point," Philip commented as he hefted pipe into place for Lawrence.

"There is always Graham," Ruby admitted.

"I know a thing or two." Lawrence tipped his head in a slight bow of farewell towards Kara as he walked back towards the fence line and he and Philip began welding the pipe into place.

"Glad you came. Sorry again that I didn't call you."

"Lawrence briefly told me what happened. I can't believe that guy came back to hassle you."

"Yes, well, thankfully Law was there to help me." Ruby watched as he worked, his back bent over his project as he diligently and skillfully made the cuts for the fence.

"Come on, the girls are at the house." Ruby started to walk away, watching as both Philip and Lawrence raised their welding helmets to survey their work and look it over. "You know what? Hold on one second." Ruby walked over towards Lawrence.

He glanced up from his work in time for her to remove his helmet from the top of his head and wrap her arms around his neck in a tight hug. His eyes flashed to Philip in surprise before he wrapped his arms around Ruby's tiny waist. "Thanks, Law." She pulled away shyly, his helmet still in her hands. "I don't think I've expressed how grateful I am for your intervention last night."

"Don't mention it." He straightened to his full height as he tapped his knuckle to her chin. "You know I'd do anything for you, right?"

"I do. And I never thank you for it."

"You don't have to." He nodded over her shoulder towards Kara. "Y'all better head on, sparks are about to fly again." He motioned towards Philip who leaned against the next post, feet crossed at the ankles as if he had all the time in the world.

"I owe you," Ruby said and squeezed his arm in thanks. "Let's go fishing this week. Just the two of us."

"We haven't done that in a while." He rubbed his sleeve over his forehead. "Usual spot?"

She nodded.

"Alright. Give me another hour to finish this section. I'll come to the house and get you."

"Not today, Law." She laughed. "But this week. Let's do it Wednesday evening."

"Alright, Wednesday then."

He watched as she and Kara headed back towards the house.

"When was the last time you two fished together?" Philip asked.

"About ten years ago." Lawrence shook his head as if he didn't understand her request and Philip grinned. "What?"

Philip removed his gloves and stuffed them in his back pocket. "Why don't we just stop where we're at and you take her to the tank now?"

"Because we don't have much left and she specifically just said not right now." Lawrence pointed at the work that lay ahead of them.

"Lawrence—" Philip shook his head in deepest sympathy. "A beautiful woman, who is deeply thankful for your presence here on Earth, just asked you to go fishing with her. You don't choose to weld fence when that happens. Because trust me, it doesn't happen every day."

"It's just Ruby."

"Oh, I guess you're right. I guess she can just call Jimmy to take her, then."

Lawrence's back stiffened. "That coward did nothing last night. I mean, I like the guy, but cowardice is a deep character flaw."

Philip's brows rose at his brother's harsh tone. "You're right. And he's also not the one Ruby wants to spend time with. Perhaps you should open your eyes, little brother. Ruby, even if she is *just* Ruby, is a beautiful, sweet, hard working woman, and a phenomenal catch. If you go fishing with any woman, or *for* any woman, she'd be a prize catch. Don't rule her out."

"It's just fishing. And I *am* going to take her fishing. Get your ears checked, Phil." Lawrence, confused, walked his torch over to the bed of his truck. "Besides, I'm not looking for a woman in my life. I have Julia, Alice, Helena, and Annie." He grinned. "I don't think I need another one."

"Cute." Philip rolled his eyes.

"I'll be sure to remind you of that on Ruby's wedding day when she's marrying someone else."

"Marriage?" Lawrence's eyes bulged. "Whoa, Phil, I think we are all a long ways from that. Well, except Graham and Julia."

"Speak for yourself." Philip crossed his arms over his chest.

"Oh really? You're going to ask Helena?"

"Not right now, but it's on my mind, because a woman like Helena doesn't come along twice in life. I'm not stupid." He narrowed his gaze on Lawrence.

Annie's car appeared up the drive and Lawrence groaned. "Here we go. I don't know who told her, but even if I wanted to take Ruby fishing today, I can't now that Annie is showing up. She's going to want the scoop."

"Then rescue her from the interrogation." Philip pointed to the fishing poles that were a staple in the back of Lawrence's truck.

"Listen," Lawrence looked Philip in the eye. "You know I care about Ruby. I always have. She's one of the best people I've ever met. And I get it, romance seems to be in the air around here as one brother after another keeps tripping head over heels in love. But I don't want that right now. I didn't help Ruby last night because I'm *in* love with her. I helped her because I love her. I also would have done it for any other woman stuck in that situation, I was just angrier because it was Ruby. Slop is one of my most favorite people, but that doesn't mean I want to follow in the footsteps of Graham, Cal, and you and start dating, courting, or loving her as more than a friend."

"You act like it's just picking out an afternoon activity. Let's see, love Ruby, go fishing, or work?" Philip smirked.

"Love *is* a choice, Phil. And it's one I don't intend on making any time soon."

"That's a shame then." Philip walked towards the passenger side of the truck, tossing his welding helmet into the back seat. "Because from a man who actually knows what love is like now, I'd never go back to who I was before Helena. Never. She is the best decision and choice I have ever made." He climbed into the pickup and shut the door, signaling to Lawrence that they were both finished working for the afternoon, and whether Lawrence was ready or not, he'd be taking Ruby fishing sooner than later.

∞

"Ruby darlin'," Annie hugged her tight and gently rocked her side to side. "I tell you I don't like it one bit when you have to leave that diner so late at night by yourself."

"I'm okay, Annie."

"Well, yes, this time. Thank goodness Lawrence was there. Sweet boy." Annie released her and hugged the other women, including Kara, before she sat on the edge of the couch with nervous energy. She hopped to her feet as the screen door opened and Philip emerged, hat in hand, ready to claim Helena for the rest of the day.

"Already?" Helena asked.

He nodded. "Lawrence called it quits for the day a little earlier than planned."

"Oh." Disappointment laced her words and Philip's easy smile told everyone he didn't mind her visiting a bit longer.

"You know what? I haven't checked in with Hayes yet. I need to go do that. You mind hanging out a little longer?"

Her eyes sparkled at him and she nodded her head emphatically. "I'd like that."

"Annie." He reached over and squeezed the woman's hand.

"I just love a roughened palm." Annie patted his hand before releasing it. "The sign of a hardworking man." She winked. "Now, Philip, Helena is going to ride with me to town."

His brows rose along with everyone else's. "Is she?" he asked.

"Yes. I'm kidnapping all these gorgeous women and taking them to my house. We are going to feast like goddesses and pamper ourselves. Henry is at the Legion for the day and probably won't be home until late. So I've got the entire place to myself, and I'd like to spend time with my girls." Henry's being 'at the Legion' meant he was playing Bingo at the VFW for the day and most of the evening.

"That sounds wonderful, Annie." Julia stood. "I'll message the boys and let them know they're on their own for lunch today."

Philip saw Helena's interest at Annie's invitation and Ruby knew he'd give her a girl's day even though he wanted to spend time with her as well. "Alright. I'll swing by later this evening."

"No, you will swing by in the mornin'," Annie corrected him. "We're having a slumber party." She danced in her seat and the women laughed.

"Sounds like you're on a mission, Annie." He kissed her cheek. "I learned a long time ago not to stand in your way."

"Wise boy." She shooed him towards the door. "Now get. And you tell those brothers of yours not to be callin' or textin' every five minutes. I'll return their women eventually."

He laughed. "Yes ma'am." He walked over and kissed Helena goodbye, her hand lingering on his cheek as she soaked him in a moment longer. He turned his head and kissed the palm of her hand before pulling away and heading out the door.

Annie clapped her hands. "Alright, girls. Pack a bag. We've got loads of fun to have. Kara, honey, do you have clothes with you?"

"I brought a bag to crash at Ruby's, so yes ma'am, I do."

"Good. You're coming too." She swatted Ruby's thigh. "And you, little one?"

"I'll have to swing by the house but won't take long."

"Alright. Well, get a head start then." She nodded towards the door. "And then meet us at the house."

Ruby complied and motioned for Kara to be her ride. Lawrence had driven her to the ranch the night before.

"Julia. Alice." She studied the two women. "Pack some things. And Helena," She smiled. "well, we're already roomies for the weekend so you're all set." Annie hopped to her feet. "I'm so excited. Helena, honey, you ride with Julia and Al. I'm going to swing by the store for a few things and then I'll be at the house."

"You sure you want all of us?" Ruby asked.

"Oh honey, I have *lived* for this day." Annie gave Ruby's shoulders a squeeze. "Now, don't think we are done discussin' your woes from last night, but I want us to do it over nail polish and wine."

Ruby rolled her eyes.

"Don't you dare, Ruby Cole. You know I have to hear it from the horse's mouth. I will *not* rely on hearsay when it comes to one of my little ducklings."

"I understand." Ruby waved to the other women and she and Kara hurried towards Kara's car. "When Annie is on a mission…"

"I like her." Kara smirked. "She's sassy."

"Oh, you have no idea," Ruby warned with a smile.

H

Chapter Nine

"Here's the thing," Lawrence spoke through his speaker for hands-free calling while driving. "I finally have the time to go buy groceries. So I'm headed to Sheffield and doin' it right instead of darting down to the gas station for a gallon of milk. I'm not, however, driving to Sheffield to run everyone else's errands, Graham." He paused and then sighed. "Your fiancé works in Sheffield, Graham. Julia can pick it up Monday. Besides, I don't even think that place is open today." He listened a moment longer. "Right... well, send Seth. I'm not doing it. I've got other things to do. Later." He hung up, not really having much to do other than grocery shopping, but he didn't want to spend all day in Sheffield.

He parked his truck in a prized second spot from the front and tipped his hat to the elderly woman greeting customers as they walked inside the store. He grabbed a cart and headed towards the back of the store to work his way towards the front. He had a list, mentally, of what all he needed, but he found himself tossing a few rogue purchases into his cart. He was a sucker when it came to potato chips and dips. He could eat an entire tub of French onion dip if he wasn't careful. However, his lack of self-control did not stop him from buying two tubs of it, along with some ranch dip as well. He'd blame Seth for eating it if he burned through it too quick and felt gluttonous. He swiveled around an elderly couple parked in the middle of the aisle and spotted the entertainment section of the store. Romance seemed to be everywhere as a movie display held various romance titles. He rolled on past until an idea struck him. He backpedaled and glanced over the covers and grabbed two movies that boasted epic taglines and what he considered the most handsome of couples on the front and tossed them into his cart. He then wound his way through the store gathering the rest of his list.

He'd treated himself to an unhealthy feast of a Philly cheesesteak sandwich from one of the local sandwich shops and headed back towards the ranch. He liked getting away from the property every once in a while, but when he was done in town, he was done. He liked socializing in Parks because it was home, but Sheffield served no purpose other than a pit stop for groceries, clothes, or an occasional night out. He could only stand stopping at stoplights over and over for so long. There was only one stoplight in Parks and very little traffic. He liked that. He reached said stoplight and flipped his blinker to turn right towards Annie's house. The women would be gathered up by now, he assumed, and he had a delivery to make.

He retrieved the goodies and walked to the front door. Normally one to just walk inside and kick off his boots, he didn't want to intrude on what was a precious moment for Annie. So instead, he knocked, which felt weird, but polite.

He could hear her laughing as she walked to the door. Surprise lit her face when she saw him. "Lawrence."

"Hey Annie, is Ruby here yet?"

"She is." Her eyes darted to the bags in his hands.

"Well, can I speak to her?"

"Sure, but don't think you're coming into the house and interrupting our time together. You'll never leave, and I wouldn't have the heart to force you to."

He chuckled. "You're right about that. I'll wait right here."

"Good man. Ruby!" sShe called and walked back into the house, leaving the door open.

Ruby hurried around the corner and froze when she saw Lawrence. "Hey."

"Hey." He extended the two grocery bags her direction.

"What's this?"

"Well, I figure no girls' night is complete without sappy movies, wine, chocolate, and popcorn, so I thought I'd grab some while in town."

She peeked into the bags and smiled up at him. "This was sweet, Law. Thanks."

He shrugged, uncomfortable, and wishing he'd just left it on the steps and ran for it.

"I'd invite you in, but—"

"I have already been warned I cannot step foot inside."

Her light fluttering giggle twisted his heart. And he had the sudden urge to run his hand over her short-cropped hair. He did that a lot when he saw her. It was just a habit, but his sudden *need* to do it surprised him. "Well," He cleared his throat. "I need to head back to the ranch."

"Right." She leaned against the door jam.

"You good?" he asked.

"Yes."

"You'd tell me if you weren't, right?"

"Yes." She reached for his hand and gave it a reassuring squeeze, but he held fast when she started to release her grip. "Was there something else, Law?"

He stepped closer to her and her head tilted back to stare up at him, her gaze swirling with confusion and trepidation. He brushed a gentle finger over her soft cheek. Her breath caught and he knew he'd kiss her if he didn't back away. But he felt trapped, ensnared by her electric eyes and vulnerability. He felt unstable, jittery, and a bit foggy brained as he brushed his thumb over the top of her fingers.

"Law?" she asked quietly, her voice slightly shaking as he inched a little closer.

"I'll see you Wednesday," he mumbled and quickly backed away, turning without glancing behind him, and hurried away from Annie's before he royally screwed up and kissed her. "Dang Philip and his talk of love," he grumbled. "Stupid, stupid, stupid." He didn't want to have feelings towards Ruby. None. At all. Zero. But dang it all, he knew he did. And now he was going to have to sort that out.

∞

"What goodies did Lawrence bring you?" Annie asked and had all the other women glancing up at Ruby's stoic expression. Her hands were slack, and the bags just hung loosely on her fingers.

"Slop?" Alice asked.

"Are you okay, Ruby?" Julia asked.

She nodded and then looked to the door. "That was the weirdest thing."

Helena and Annie exchanged grins.

"Oh?" Annie asked innocently. "Is Lawrence okay?"

"Yeah, I mean, he seemed to be." She held up the bags and shook away the odd interaction she'd just had with Lawrence. Her heart was still recovering at his closeness. *Had he considered kissing her?* That's what it felt like, but that couldn't be. It was Lawrence. He flirted, he teased, he protected, but he never kissed her. She'd admit she'd been thinking about it since Alice brought it up, and she'd also admit she was a bit curious about what it would feel like to kiss Law, but that was just silly notions and 'what ifs.' She wasn't going to actually follow through. But when he'd looked down at her, his blue eyes soft and focused on her, she'd felt that familiar flutter in her chest, the twisting in her stomach, and the tingle in her toes that only came from recognition on a whole new level.

"Sooooo… what's in the bags?" Alice interrupted her thoughts, and she dipped her hand in one. "Wine." She withdrew two bottles and handed them to Helena. "Chocolate." She tossed two big packages of various chocolate candies towards Alice. "Popcorn." She tossed that to Julia and then reached into to grab the movies. "And chick flicks." She giggled on the last one, thinking of Lawrence buying such sappy movies.

"Wow." Alice reached for the movies. "Way to go, Law." She held up his choices and all the women approved.

"That was sweet of him." Julia beamed as she headed to the kitchen to pop some popcorn.

"Don't forget the butter!" Annie called after her.

"I'm blown away." Ruby eased onto the sofa next to Kara. "It's unlike him to spend money on such stuff."

"He wanted us all to have a lovely night. Deep down all the boys have sweet hearts. They just don't always show them off," Annie stated proudly.

"That is a true statement," Alice agreed. "It's weird when they do, but I have to admit, I sure do love it when Cal is sweet on me. I never in my life thought I would want flowers until he had a bouquet delivered to me at the clinic. I felt like a million bucks."

"She gloated all afternoon," Julia confirmed from the door of the kitchen.

"It's true," Alice confirmed unashamedly.

"Philip leaves me little love notes tucked away in my work bag or in my car whenever he's in town, so when he leaves, I'll find them throughout the week." Helena gleamed.

Annie placed her hand on her heart. "Isn't that the sweetest thing?"

"What about Graham, Julia?" Helena asked.

Julia held up her finger and darted into the kitchen, the sounds of her opening the microwave and preparing popcorn filtered in the room along with the warm, buttery scent. She returned and sighed as she sat on the loveseat by Alice, who fisted a handful of the hot snack immediately.

"He sends me sweet texts or sometimes I'll come home and there's a fresh bouquet of wildflowers waiting for me in the guesthouse."

"Wow." Ruby looked to Kara. "I had no idea the boys had this in them."

"Oh, come now." Annie waved away her comment. "Surely you did. Do you not remember your junior prom?"

Ruby flushed crimson. "Can we please not talk about that?"

"Oh, right." Alice snapped her fingers. "I forgot about that."

"What? What happened?" Julia asked.

"I want to know too." Kara eagerly accepted a handful of popcorn as well and sat back in the cushions as they all looked to Annie to continue her story.

"Well, Ruby was of age to go to the prom. See only juniors and seniors are allowed to go."

"Of age." Alice laughed at the terminology, receiving a frown from Annie. She cleared her throat. "Go on."

"Her grandmomma made the most beautiful dress for her. Do you still have it, Ruby?" Annie asked and was pleased at Ruby's nod. "Oh, it was the most beautiful color, almost iridescent. Ruby looked gorgeous in it."

Ruby's embarrassment turned to warmth as Annie continued.

"But I'm getting ahead of myself." Annie backtracked. "Prom was coming up and Ruby was excited she could finally go."

"But I wasn't asked by anyone."

"No date?" Helena asked in surprise.

"Nope. And not even the groups of girls going together asked me to join." She rolled her eyes.

"But no matter," Annie continued. "She wanted to go and so her grandmomma and me set about getting her ready." She reached over and squeezed Ruby's hand. "We had such fun, didn't we?"

"Yes, we did." Ruby, not revealing it was one of her most cherished memories, kept her voice quiet. That was two weeks before her grandmother's passing, and none of them knew that that night would be one of her fondest memories and that prom dress would be one of her most treasured possessions.

"Anyway, the night came, and we dolled Ruby up, got her dressed, and we were going to take her up to the school. When we opened the front door, every single Hastings brother lined the sidewalk. And each of them held a flower." Annie placed a hand on her heart. "Even Lawrence, Hayes, and Clint who all had their own dates for the prom waiting on them. They still showed up. And Graham, Cal, and Philip, even though they were graduated, stood proudly, dressed in their finest, holding a flower for Ruby. Seth, still in junior high at the time, was the first one on the front steps, and he escorted Ruby down the sidewalk like a wedding march to the car, each brother giving her a flower."

"That is the sweetest thing." Kara looked to her friend and Ruby nodded.

"Oh my goodness, was Lawrence's date mad," Annie chuckled. "Apparently he didn't even buy her a corsage."

"So how was prom?" Julia asked.

"It was great." Ruby smiled. "Lawrence and I danced pretty much the entire time together."

"Then why didn't he just ask you to be his date?" Helena asked.

"Reagan Little had her claws in him."

"That girl had her claws in every young man," Annie mumbled, and Alice hooted in laughter.

Ruby smirked. "Besides, Lawrence was just her ticket into the prom. She was a sophomore. She needed an upper classman to take her in order to go, so she pretty much did her own thing once they got there."

"So Lawrence made Ruby's night magical instead," Annie finished.

"I wouldn't go that far. You're giving him way too much credit." Ruby laughed. "He just danced with me. I also danced with Hayes," she added for good measure.

"But Lawrence is the one who brought you home," Annie pointed out.

"He did," Ruby confirmed.

"Did he kiss you?" Kara asked.

Ruby shook her head. "No."

"No kiss?" Julia, Alice, and Helena repeated in unison and a laugh burst forth from Ruby.

"We were just friends," she reminded them.

"So you and Law have never kissed?" Alice asked.

"No."

"Wow." Alice looked dumbfounded. "I sort of thought that ship had sailed a long time ago."

"We are friends," Ruby stated again.

"So? Cal and I were friends growing up and I'm pretty sure we kissed in the hay barn once to just 'try it out'."

"Who knew that one day you'd want to kiss him even more?" Julia asked.

"Not me, that is for sure. I'm so glad—"

"You listened to me?" Julia finished her sentence.

"Don't gloat, Julia."

Julia gloated anyway and had the other women laughing.

"So that's the story," Ruby concluded. "The Hastings brothers are sweet when they want to be."

"I don't even know them that well and I think I'm in love with all of them." Kara chuckled and had Annie straightening in her chair with pride.

"Don't say that too loud," Alice warned. "Or Annie will have one picked out for you."

"So, Lawrence comes to your rescue, he delivers you a bag of goodies for your girls' night, and he's taking you fishing on Wednesday..." Kara bit back a smile as Ruby fidgeted.

"Fishing?" Annie asked. "I didn't know this."

"We fish all the time."

"No you don't." Alice looked perplexed.

"Well, we have in the past. We're going Wednesday. Just for fun."

Julia's small squeal of excitement had Helena beaming as well. "It's happening again."

Ruby waved her hands. "No, it isn't."

"Don't you see?" Julia asked. "He's all confused about how he feels for you now. This exact thing happened between Calvin and Alice. Cal had to sort it out and Alice denied it as long as she could, and now look at them." Julia motioned to her lovesick friend who, despite her unladylike posture while draped on the couch, nodded around a mouthful of popcorn.

"It's one of the first times I've let my pride go and just accepted—"

"That I was right," Julia finished quickly again and received a kernel of popcorn tossed into her hair.

"Just don't rule him out, Slop," Alice suggested. "I know it's weird to even think of something beyond friendship with Law. Trust me, I do. And not to sound too gushy, but if I'd let Cal slip through my fingers, it would have been the worst move of my life. So just take it one step at a time."

"I'm not taking any steps," Ruby's voice rose. "I have no intention of seeing where it goes with Lawrence. We're friends. He was there when I needed him. Again," she added. "But that doesn't mean I want more than that. Besides, I've been dating Jimmy."

"You're still going to after that night at the diner?"

Ruby could tell that Alice was not the only female in the room who didn't like that idea. "Maybe."

"Jimmy wasn't the man who stood up for you," Alice stated.

"And he's not the one who took you home to care for you," Helena added.

"Or the one who brought you a bag of goodies to your girls' night 'just because,'" Julia added.

"*Or* the one who comes to the diner multiple times a week just to see you," Kara finished.

"He comes to the diner because he doesn't want to cook for himself."

"Half the time, he doesn't even eat," Kara pointed out. "I've noticed."

"Oh really?" Julia crossed her arms over her chest as if trying to decide how much to read into that small tidbit of news.

"He's protective. He checks on me. So does Clint. Clint is there at least twice a week. Philip is there almost every other day. Cal swings by once a week. Seth comes in every now and then. Hayes and Graham less so, but when I need them... it's not special attention from Lawrence. It's just what the boys do. And I don't want these notions planted in my head or then I will feel weird around him."

"Trust me," Julia pointed to the chick flick movies on the side table. "Notions are already in his head, so you best prepare yourself."

Choosing to ignore Julia's comment and those of the other women, Ruby decided to just appreciate Lawrence for his friendship. They'd

always seen about one another. It was a given.
Nothing would change that. And she didn't want
their friendship compromised by meddling and
misplaced hopes.

H

Chapter Ten

He sat on the stone bridge he and his brothers had built over a decade ago, his boots dangling over the side and just above the creek on the side that fed into a larger tank, or pond, of water. The water level was already lowering due to the summer heat and not enough rain, but they still had a couple of weeks' worth for decent fishing or swimming before the level dropped too low. Lawrence reached into the metal can beside him and fished out a wriggling worm and baited his hook. Ruby hadn't shown up yet, but he figured he'd get started. Even if she didn't show up, he was bound to catch something for his supper. Hayes had helped him find worms earlier in the day, and he felt equipped enough to at least bring home a couple of fish for a meal.

"Any luck so far?" Ruby asked, walking up with her own pole in hand, wearing short denim cut-offs and a bright blue tank top.

"Just a couple of bites." He cast his line out in front of him, the orange bobber floating on the soft ripples.

Ruby eased down beside him, her purple sneakers worn from miles of walking at the diner.

He moved the can of bait between them.

"Ooo, these are good ones." She held up a thick juicy worm. "Hayes helped you, didn't he?"

"Yep."

"How does he always find the good ones?"

Lawrence grinned as he watched her bait her own hook without even the slightest hesitation, as though she'd fished every weekend.

"Have you been out here long?"

"Not really, about a half hour or so." He reeled in his line and cast it back out again. "I only have a couple of hours and then I have to be cleaned up and over at the stables."

"For what?"

"Apparently Graham and Julia are having engagement photos taken today."

"Oh, that's right." Ruby nodded in recognition. "She mentioned that at girls' night."

"Kara runnin' the diner tonight?"

"For a bit. I'll head back up there when we are done. So why do you have to be at the photo shoot?"

"Julia wanted photos with all of us."

"That's nice."

He shrugged. "I don't really feel like gettin' fancy for photos, but Graham insisted we be there at five. Something about the right lighting and wanting the sunset to be included in the photos."

"It will look stunning, I have no doubt." Ruby cast her line into the water. "So, how've you been, Law?"

He smirked. "Good. Why?"

"Just making conversation." Ruby reeled a couple of a turns and then let her line rest.

He studied the side of her face a minute. "You itchin' to ask me something?"

She looked at him. "No, why?"

"That's usually the question someone asks when they're trying to dig for info on something."

"Can I not just be interested in how you've been?"

He eyed her a minute longer and noticed her nervous hands as she tightened her grip on her rod. "Sure," he replied. "I'm doing fine. You?"

"Can't complain."

He chuckled. "I guess that's good." His line jerked, his bobber disappearing beneath the water a second before he started reeling in his catch.

"Way to go." Excited, Ruby ignored her own line to see what Lawrence caught.

"A simple cat." He removed the catfish from the hook and attached it to the stringer line he'd prepared, letting it linger in the cool water while they continued fishing. He baited his next hook and felt Ruby staring at him. When he glanced her direction, she diverted her gaze to her bobber. "Something on your mind, Slop?" he asked.

"No. What? Why? No," she fumbled.

He smirked. "Okay... you seem a bit distracted. What's on your mind?"

"I'd rather not say."

"Why?"

"Because it's a lot."

KATHARINE E. HAMILTON

"I've got two ears for that purpose. When one gets tired of listening, the other one steps up its game. Now, talk."

"You remember our junior prom?" she asked.

His brows rose at the randomness of her line of thinking. "Yes..." he replied. "Why is that on your mind?"

"Oh, Annie shared about it at girls' night the other night."

"Wait," Lawrence held up her hand for her to stop. "isn't there some sort of code that what happens at girls' night stays at girls' night?"

She swatted his hand down. "I'm serious, Law. Do you remember?"

"Well, yeah, why wouldn't I? We had fun."

"Yeah, we did." Her smile turned reminiscent as she studied her line. She'd lost her bait minutes ago, but he dared not interrupt her. "Why did she bring it up?"

"Oh, Al and Julia were gushing about Graham and Cal, and Annie had to point out how fabulous all of you were."

He grinned. "She's our biggest champion. She also brags on us more in private than she ever does to our face."

"Gotta keep your pride in check," Ruby replied.

"Exactly." He shifted on the bridge and angled his body towards hers. "So, she was promoting our good qualities for what purpose? Kara?"

"Me," Ruby clarified. "I guess she'd thought I'd forgotten how much you boys have done for me over the years."

"And vice versa." He added.

"Yeah, but the focus was on you boys."

"Why though?"

Her hesitancy had him worried. "What's going on, Ruby?"

She turned to him, her eyes glassy as if she might burst into tears at any moment. "I'm so confused, Law."

"About what?" He reached a hand towards her face and she avoided his touch.

"You."

"Me? What about me?" He was attempting to follow the line of conversation, but he was failing miserably. All he could tell was that he'd upset her somehow, and that didn't sit well with him.

"We're good friends, aren't we?"

"Of course. The best," he assured her. "Always will be. No matter what. Why? What was said?"

She groaned and reeled in her line, even more annoyed when she spotted her empty hook. She set her rod on the bridge.

"Where are you going?"

"I-I think I just need to go." Her voice quivered and he sat stunned.

"Sloppy, wait." He rushed to stand and snatched her arm before she could dart away, her face red in embarrassment. "What is going on?" he asked again with a little more force. "Look, come here." He pointed to his boots and took them off his feet, followed by his socks as he set them aside. He motioned for her to do the same. She obliged, confused as to what he was going to have her do. He sat on the bridge and slid slowly into the water, soaking his clothes, the water level coming up to his mid-chest. "Get in."

She shook her head.

"Slop, get in. I'm going to show you something."

She hesitated a second longer before slipping into the water, his arms helping sort her, knowing she'd barely have her head above the water due to the depth and her short frame. He tugged for her to float under the bridge with him. "Let's see..." His eyes roamed over the underside of the stone bridge until they landed on a rock just above the water line. LH and RC were carved into the surface. "Remember this?"

A soft smile tilted her lips. "That was a long time ago."

"Fifteen years ago, actually. Remember when we did it?"

She nodded solemnly.

"It was the day of your grandmomma's funeral," Lawrence reminded her. "You'd come down here to the creek to get away from the crowd up at the house. I found you sittin' here on the bridge."

"That was a rough day." Her voice was clouded with grief he knew would never fully go away. He knew that grief, having lost both his parents at a young age as well.

"And what did we promise one another?" he asked her.

"That'd we always be there for each other."

"Exactly." He brushed a thumb over their initials, and she did the same before turning to him. "So what is wrong, Slop? Because you know you can tell me anything."

She reached towards him, her arm winding around his neck bringing her close to him. Her eyes landed on his lips and he thought for a brief moment she was going to kiss him, until he realized she was probably just tired of tiptoeing in the water and bobbing beneath the surface. But then she did. Her lips, uncertain, trembled against his. Her kiss was soft, quiet, and completely disarming. Her fingers tickled the back of his neck. She pulled away, resting her forehead against his. "I'm sorry," she whispered. "I just—"

He didn't let her finish, but instead pressed his lips to hers again, only this time he held the reins. She responded, her other arm looping around his neck, his arms around her waist to keep her above the water. If he was finally going to kiss Ruby, he was going to do it right. He'd been thinking about it for weeks, and if he were truly being honest, he'd thought about it multiple times over the years. This was his moment, and he wasn't going to blow it. Whether she accepted him as more than a friend didn't matter now, because he was bound and determined to ruin any thoughts she might have towards other men. He was in this for the end game. He wanted Ruby for himself. He loved her. He'd always loved her, and no other man would ever love her like he did. And he wanted to prove that to her. So he kissed her with every thought, feeling, and fiber of his being until he felt her gently press a hand against his chest to nudge him back. Breathless, he closed his eyes. He felt her tender kisses on his forehead, cheeks, and corners of his mouth before she laid another long, satisfying kiss on his lips. She pulled away. "Maybe that should stay under here with the rock."

"It doesn't have to." His voice was rasped with emotion as he searched her beautiful face. "Ruby—"

She pulled away from his embrace and treaded back a few arm lengths from him. "Let's just let it soak in for a bit Lawrence."

He rubbed a hand over his mouth and face as he nodded. "Got it." Annoyed, he waded to the bank and climbed out, ringing water from his shirt. "I should go get ready for pictures."

"Lawrence, I didn't mean I didn't want this." She swam towards the edge and climbed out of the water, standing toe to toe with him. "I just... I want to be sure."

"I get it." He ran a hand over the back of his neck as she grabbed his other one and held it in both her own.

Her eyes searched his face. "Do you?"

"Yes." He sighed and gently tapped her chin with his knuckle. He withdrew from her grasp so he could think straight and avoid her alarmingly vulnerable and beautiful eyes. "Just... let me know, okay?"

He heard her soft whisper of "I will" as he walked towards his house, leaving his fishing gear, but not the memory of their kiss, behind.

∞

Ruby mopped up a spill, the fourth one of the evening, as Kara hurried by her carrying three large platters to an awaiting table.

She hurried the mop bucket back into the kitchen and towards the back of the diner in the washroom and washed her hands.

"You're makin' a habit of that." Sal nodded towards the washroom.

"Seems like everyone is jittery tonight and spilling drinks." She exited the kitchen and walked to the bar. Jimmy sat in his usual spot. Things had definitely changed between them since the night of the crazy man threatening her. He wasn't as flirty with her or attentive. He was still nice and kind, but not near as intentional as he had been. Though, after her afternoon of kissing Lawrence, she was somewhat grateful. Her heart had been tied up all evening thinking back to that moment under the bridge. The last time she'd ever considered falling in love with Lawrence Hastings was when she was seven years old and desperately wished to be a part of the Hastings family. She desired family as a kid, and the Hastings brothers embodied that. So her simple logic was just to marry Lawrence and then she'd always have a family to be a part of. A sad notion, she realized years later, and was thankful she'd never confessed that to Law. And she was a part of the family, even without marriage to one of the brothers, and for that, she was beyond thankful to the man upstairs. They'd been a tremendous blessing to her over the years. They found solace in one another at losing parents and grandparents. They shared the responsibility of taking care of Annie and Henry as they aged, a responsibility they all honored and appreciated. And they loved one another, unconditionally, like only families could. But now her heart wanted something different. She wanted Lawrence, and not just as her friend and partner in crime, but as her love. As someone she could come home to and kiss in the evenings, cook breakfast for, raise a family with. She was head over heels in love with Lawrence Hastings. She wasn't quite sure how it happened, but it did, long before that kiss under the bridge. She just hadn't recognized it for what it was. Maybe it was when they'd carved their initials into a stone at seventeen or when he'd smiled across the room from her in first grade boasting a missing tooth, courtesy of Clint. Her heart cherished every memory with Lawrence. Every moment in his presence always made her feel welcome and noticed and safe. He was charming, funny, and slightly rambunctious so that he kept you on your toes. And he had a heart of gold for the ones he loved. She loved everything about him. How had she missed it?

Kara walked up and removed the towel from Ruby's hands causing her to start. "You alright? You've been distracted all evening."

"I'm fine," Ruby assured her.

"You sure?"

"I kissed Lawrence," Ruby blurted, several patrons looking up at her announcement. She cast a nervous glance towards Jimmy, but he'd already left.

"Oh really?" Kara asked with a slight smile. "And?"

"And I think I'm in love with him," Ruby continued and then felt her face grow pale.

Kara reached out a hand and led her to a stool to sit. "You look like you're about to faint."

"I think I am." Ruby held a hand to her head. "How have I not realized it before?"

Kara's smile turned tender as she squeezed Ruby's hand with hers. "Sometimes we get so caught up in the day to day of life's routine that we lose sight of people or things right in front of us. But that's okay. Because sooner or later we recognize the moments and people that are important to us. Sounds like you've had that happen."

"Yeah." Ruby looked at her hands in her lap. "Well, now it's all I can think about and I don't know what to do about it."

"Does he know?"

"I think so. I mean, I don't really know. We kissed and I sort of just ran. The thing is, I think he might feel the same way."

"Then that's exciting," Kara reassured her.

"And terrifying."

"Oh, honey." Kara brushed a hand over Ruby's silky hair. "Embrace it. Being loved by a good man is a rare thing. Treasure it."

"I just don't know how to bring it up to him again. I mean, the next time we see each other is he going to talk to me about it? Is it something we'll just mutually sweep under the rug? Or will we have the moment Alice and Cal had and just jump in and let everyone know?"

"Don't compare your story to Alice's. Lawrence is a different man and you're a different woman. Your relationship is different as well. I don't know Lawrence well, but what little I do know is that he'd cross heaven and earth for you, and you don't even have to ask. He cares for you deeply. Don't ignore what happened between the two of you. That is the worst move you could possibly make. Trust me. Tell him your feelings."

Kara patted her leg. "Take a break. Get some air. It's not busy, so I can watch this place for a bit."

Ruby stood to her feet. "Thanks, Kara. Thanks for being a good friend."

"Anytime." Kara waved her out the front door, Ruby pausing to rest a hand on a sleeping Roughneck Randy's shoulder as Porter glanced up at her. She motioned for him to follow her, the dog happily rising to his feet and walking alongside her. Instinct had her walking towards the cemetery to the familiar markers of her grandparents. She sat, Porter easing onto his haunches beside her, her hand brushing down his back in soothing strokes. This was her thinking spot. Though she knew they couldn't hear her or even respond, she still came and talked out her dilemmas and problems with them. A verbal journal invisibly marked into their headstones from years of confessions, feelings, and thoughts. Only this time, she didn't have anything to say, so she just sat, enjoyed the peace and quiet, and thought about Lawrence Hastings and her newest revelation.

H

Chapter Eleven

"I'm on my way, Annie."

Lawrence buckled his seat belt and turned the key in the ignition. "What's for supper?" He listened, his mouth watering at just the thought. "I love your chicken pot pie. See you in a few." He hung up and started his way from his house and through the ranch towards the main entrance. He paused in front of Graham's house to give a wave to Graham and Julia as they sat on the porch. Julia waved for him to stop and to hold on a minute. She darted into Graham's house and Graham advanced towards Lawrence's truck.

"Headed into town to Annie's?" Graham asked.

"Yep. Friday supper." Lawrence rubbed his stomach. "Chicken pot pie."

"Nice." Graham nodded proudly towards his house. "Julia's making some sort of chicken alfredo tonight."

"That sounds awesome."

"It probably will be."

"What's she need me to do?" Lawrence asked, and both men looked to the door as Julia hurried out carrying a freshly potted succulent plant.

"This is for Annie. She'd been wanting some cuttings of this and I just got around to it today. Do you mind?"

"Do I mind bringing Annie, the queen of all plants, a gift? No. I do not. I'll try not to take credit for it."

Julia grinned as she handed it to him through his window and he placed it on his passenger floorboard.

"Give Annie and Henry hugs for us." Julia slid her arm around Graham's waist, his brother pulling her tighter to his side, and Lawrence liked the look of them.

"You bet. See you in the morning for football." Lawrence turned down the main drive and headed towards Parks.

Tonight would be the first night he'd seen Ruby or even talked to her since their little encounter under the bridge at the creek. What was he thinking? There was nothing little about their kiss. He'd kissed her with everything he had, so her silence stung. He thought for sure she'd swing by the ranch and hash things out with him. But she hadn't. She'd stayed glued to the diner. No calls, no texts. Granted he hadn't reached out to her either, but she said she needed to sort it out, so he'd left the ball in her court. But tonight he'd get an answer one way or the other. If she avoided him, then he knew that kiss was to stay hidden beneath the bridge. If she didn't, well then, he was ready for whatever lay ahead of them.

He pulled in behind Philip's truck and shifted into park. Helena was in Midland for the weekend and Philip was already mourning not seeing her, as was evident by the texts he shot Lawrence's way earlier in the day. So he'd hang out with his brother and enjoy quality time with Annie and Henry regardless of what Ruby decided.

He walked inside, obediently removing his boots at the door and hanging his hat on the wall next to Philip's.

"In here, Lawrence!" Annie called from the kitchen.

He inhaled a deep breath before walking into the homey kitchen, the smell of sage and pie crust wafting through the air and setting his stomach to rolling in anticipation. Henry and Philip sat at the table playing a game of gin and Annie hustled around the oven checking her timer. She smiled in welcome. "Tea?"

"Yes ma'am." He walked to the pitcher she pointed to on the counter and poured himself a glass. "Ruby coming?" He kept his voice casual and was pleased when Annie didn't think anything of his comment.

"Supposed to be. She was going to come around seven, I think."

He glanced at the clock and realized he had about ten minutes before Ruby arrived. His nerves bounced inside his body, his fingers clumsy as he picked up his glass. He gripped it tighter on his walk towards the table. Philip eyed him curiously but glanced back at his cards.

"You losing?" Lawrence asked.

"Of course." Philip groaned when Henry happily declared gin and set his cards down. "And that is the sixth consecutive win for Henry."

Henry's deep chuckle had the men grinning at one another. "I think he lets me." Henry winked at Philip as he looked up at Lawrence. His face sobered instantly. "My word, boy, what's got you in a frazzle?"

Annie's head popped up then from behind the counter as she busied her hands with a salad, her eyes now scrutinizing every inch of Lawrence's face.

"Nothing." He slid into a chair at the table, everyone staring at him.

"Don't lie to me, son. I know when something's eatin' at you. What's got you gnawin' hay these days?"

Lawrence rubbed a hand over his face to give himself time to think, his palm scratching against his beard. The front door opened and closed, and Ruby's voice drifted into the house. "I'm here!"

Lawrence instantly tensed and Philip's brow tilted up as Henry bit back a grin. "I see," he whispered, focusing his attention back on shuffling the deck of cards in front of him.

She entered the kitchen in her usual whirl of activity, swooping Annie in a hug, kissing Henry's cheek, hugging Philip, and giving Lawrence a quick nod of hello before slipping to the sink to wash her hands. Annie handed her plates and Ruby brought them to the table.

"How's the diner tonight?" Annie asked.

"Not too bad, actually. I'm thankful for Kara more and more every day."

"She has been a blessing," Annie agreed. "We get to see more of you now that you can take a break from that place every once in a while."

Ruby placed the plates on the table as Henry cleared his cards and set them aside, handing them to Philip to place on the antique sideboard that nestled against the wall behind the table.

Annie brought the salad over and hurried to grab the pot pie, while Ruby dished out silverware, everyone preparing their own place setting. She'd yet to meet Lawrence's gaze. Annie settled in her chair and motioned for Ruby to have a seat. She eased onto the chair by Lawrence but seemed to sit on the opposite edge just in case she needed to make a quick escape. It irritated him.

"Philip, will you say grace?" Annie asked.

The older brother bowed his head and led them in a quick prayer of thanks before everyone started passing their plate to Annie.

"How've you been?" Lawrence whispered, his eyes focused on the plate Philip handed towards him, the pot pie's steam swirling into the air as it passed over the table.

Ruby squirmed. "Good. Busy," she replied.

"How'd the photo shoot go?" Henry asked.

"Good." Philip grinned. "Julia's got us all under her thumb. She wanted pictures of just her and

Graham and then pictures of just us brothers together. I guess she figured while she has us all wrangled together and polished up, she better make the most of it."

Henry snickered. "That girl fits this family like a glove, doesn't she? Graham could not have chosen a better find."

"I'm still perplexed how Graham of all people pulled that off," Lawrence teased.

"It was by the grace of God," Annie added, making everyone laugh. "Bless his heart. I knew one day he'd find a woman that would love that tough shell he presents to the world. What I never thought I'd see was a woman who cracks that shell from time to time."

"They're definitely good for each other." Ruby took a bite of her pot pie, Lawrence wanting to scream that they, too, were good for each other, but he let the moment pass.

"Lawrence, you kick that little brother out yet?" Henry asked.

"Not yet. Seth's got the house plans drawn and the ground cleared and leveled but work probably won't start on it for a while. Little brother realizes he has expensive taste and is wanting to save up a bit more before he takes the plunge in building."

"Well, don't let him ruin your pretty house," Annie warned.

"He's gotten better," Lawrence defended. "Still won't pick up his clothes around the place, but he's tidier in the kitchen and bathrooms, and that's a huge step."

"You're a saint to have lasted this long puttin' up with that." Annie shook her head. "That boy needs a good boot to the rear sometimes."

"He gets it," Philip and Lawrence said at the same time.

Henry chuckled again knowing it was the truth.

"Phil, how's our Helena?" Henry asked. "We were disappointed not to have her this weekend."

"She's been busy traveling her region, so she was pretty tuckered out. And I have a shipment scheduled to come in tomorrow morning so I couldn't head to Midland."

"I could have covered for you," Lawrence offered.

"I'll remember that next time."

"What's the purpose of all of you boys if you can't help each other out every now and then?" Annie asked. "Ruby too." She nodded to the spritely young woman.

The front door opened and closed.

"I wonder who is joining us." Annie stood and hustled towards the living room, her joyful greeting bringing Calvin into the room.

"Well, well, well." Henry shook his hand. "It's been a while since you've been at the table, boy. How are things with the doc?"

Cal grinned. "Good. Alice is out on call tonight and I could smell Annie's cookin' all the way at my house. Sorry I didn't call." He leaned his head back to look at Annie as she stood behind his chair. She tapped his chin lovingly. "It's a wonderful surprise. I'll get you a plate." She was quick to her task. "Any of the other boys coming?"

"Don't think so," Calvin said. "Hayes was still at the stables. He's determined to break one of those new purchases of his before December."

"That boy needs to learn to take a break." Henry shook his head. "Either that or he'll never be able to sit like a regular human being again. All those falls can't be good on a man's body."

"He can handle it." Annie slid back into her seat, noticing the silence that lingered between the usually playful Lawrence and Ruby. "Is everything okay between you two?" She asked, motioning her fork back and forth. "Y'all sure are quiet this evenin'."

"Fine," they both said.

"Y'all haven't even looked at one another. Which one of you made the other mad?"

"I'm not mad," Ruby said.

"Me either," Lawrence agreed.

"Then what is it? Because it's something, and it's disturbing the peace of my table."

Calvin shared a quick questioning glance with Philip as though they could communicate any news silently between their minds. Seemed neither of them knew anything had transpired to cause such a rift between Law and Ruby.

Ruby shoveled the last of her supper into her mouth and hopped to her feet. "I should really get back to the diner." She hurried towards the sink, Lawrence jumping to his feet.

"Ruby, wait!" She froze, a nervous hand swiping her sweeping bangs from her face. "Just, wait."

Annie eased quietly back in her chair, her eyes wide as she realized she had unearthed something more serious than she'd considered.

"Lawrence, I'm fine. I just need to go."

"No, you don't." He started to walk towards her, and she looked as if she might flee, so he stopped. "This isn't right." He moved his hand towards her and then himself. "We're always good. There's never something that's come up that we haven't dealt with. This is no different."

"I think it's very different, Law." Ruby's quiet voice twisted his heart and he prepared himself for disappointment.

"Alright. Well then, let me just say my piece and then you can decide to do what you want with it. After that, it's done, and we don't have to talk about it anymore."

She nodded hesitantly, her hands resting on the kitchen island, feeling protected by the barrier between them.

"I love you," Lawrence announced to the room. The small gasp of surprise from Annie behind him encouraged him further. "I think deep down I always have. But now I'm sayin' it, and I mean it. The other day at the bridge confirmed it even more. Now I get it, we've been friends for a long time, but you still make me nervous." He exhaled a shaky breath and held up his shaky hands. "I'm terrified right now at how you'll respond. My heart twists when you look at me. It squeezes in my chest when I get the rare chance at holdin' you. I come to the diner so much because I vowed years ago that I'd keep an eye on you. But what I didn't realize until the other day is that I like that job. I don't want anyone else to have that job. I want to be the man that looks out for you, loves you, keeps you safe. It's always been my role, and I don't want anyone else having it. Call me selfish, I don't care, but you're mine, Ruby Cole, and you always have been."

A tear slid down Ruby's cheek and she quickly swiped it away on a sniffle.

"Now," Lawrence walked around the island towards her and tilted her chin to look up at him. "what say you?"

∞

"And then what happened?" Julia took a sip of her wine as Annie relayed the story to her and Alice over drinks on the front porch of the main house as the brothers duked it out in the yard for their weekly flag football match. Ruby had yet to arrive and spill the beans, but a beaming Lawrence warmed everyone's heart as he seemed more chipper than usual.

"She said she loved him too." Annie's hand rested on her heart. "It was the loveliest moment I've witnessed in a long time."

"I knew Slop would come around." Alice grinned as Ruby's little car wound down the dirt drive and she stepped out. "I think your ears were burnin'," Alice called to her.

Ruby hustled towards them, careful to avoid the diving bodies of Seth and Hayes as Graham threw a pass their direction. When they'd rerouted, she hurried towards the steps. "Oh yeah? Why am I the current topic?"

Julia nodded towards Lawrence as he took a full-on tackle from Clint and tossed his brother over his head and onto his back. The women grimaced. "That's going to leave a mark!" Alice cheered and Lawrence flashed her a thumbs up, his eyes landing on Ruby, and his smile widening even further.

He jogged their direction, taking the jeers from his brothers at leaving his position as he reached the top step. He wound his hand around her waist and pulled Ruby towards him, kissing her soundly on the mouth.

"Well, well, well..." Julia fanned herself and caught Graham's amused glance. She winked at him as Alice took a long sip of her water bottle.

"I need to cool off," Alice mumbled, making Julia laugh and breaking the moment between Ruby and Lawrence.

"I've wanted to do that all mornin'." Lawrence kissed her quickly one more time, the football nailing him in the back as Calvin waited, hands on his hips, for his brother to resume his position. Lawrence pulled away and held up his hands. "Sorry, I'm coming." He yelled over his shoulder. "I just can't stop." He tapped Ruby's chin as he headed back down the stairs. He turned and walked backwards so he could keep his eyes on her. "I think I'm gonna have to marry you so I can do that whenever I want, Ruby Cole."

Ruby leaned on the porch railing with a satisfied smile. "Maybe you should, Lawrence Hastings."

"Then it's settled." Lawrence grinned. "You and me, darlin', for always." He pointed at her and winked when she nodded, turning his attention to an approaching Graham as his brother stuffed the football into his arms and ordered him take over as quarterback. "Get after it, Romeo."

∞

Three Weeks Later

"Dress shopping this weekend. You in?" Julia asked as Ruby refilled her soda to-go cup at the bar.

"Sure. Is your mom coming into town?"

"Yep. Annie, Helena, and Alice are coming too. I want all of you there."

"Then I'd be happy to." Ruby grinned. "Are you nervous?"

"Not really." Julia leaned forward, her voice soft. "Are you?" She nodded to the simple diamond ring that graced Ruby's left hand.

"I'm still getting used to it." Ruby sighed contentedly. "It will be a while before Lawrence and I tie the knot. For one thing, I don't want to interfere or steal the attention away from you and Graham."

Julia waved away that concern, but Ruby pressed on. "I mean it. Graham deserves his moment. And you too, but Graham has been there for all of us through the years. For once, I want him to be the center of everyone's focus for a bit."

"That's sweet of you." Julia reached for Ruby's hand and looked at her ring again. "Isn't it amazing how Lawrence just *happened* to have this lying around?"

"I thought he was somewhat teasing that day when he said he was going to marry me. But when he showed up at the diner with all the brothers to help him make his proposal, my heart... well, I thought it was going to burst."

"He told Graham and me he bought this ring after he helped you out that night after the crazy construction guy incident."

"What?" Ruby asked.

"Said he knew he wanted to always protect you, and that the more he thought about it, the more he realized he loved you. So he went 'ring lookin,'" Julia air-quoted. "I guess he found what he was looking for and kept it on hand for when he'd finally come to full terms with his heart."

"That guy." Ruby shook her head and nibbled back a smile.

"The Hastings boys are quite an interesting bunch." Julia released Ruby's hand. "I'm excited for you, Ruby. I'm excited about everything these days, it seems, but I'm so excited that we'll be sisters."

"Likewise. Though you haven't seen anything yet, Julia, I warn you."

Laughing, Julia stood to her feet. "Bring it on." She shouldered her purse. "Thanks for the soda. I'm going to walk back over to the feed store and see if Graham is done hassling Philip."

"Must have been important for Graham to come all the way to town."

"It wasn't." Julia waved her hand away. "Clint just ordered the wrong protein or something, so Graham felt compelled to take care of it himself and in person."

Ruby rolled her eyes. "Oh, Graham."

"Gotta' love 'im." Julia grinned. "And I do," she finished chipperly. "See you this weekend. We'll pick you up on the way unless you're at the ranch for whatever reason."

"I'll probably be here. Randy's informed me I've been galivantin' around too much and that he misses me."

"Well, you can tell Randy that he's not the one who put that ring on your finger, so he will just have to get used to you taking breaks and spending time with a handsome cowboy."

Ruby's face lit up. "I'll do that. See you later, Julia."

Julia waved over her shoulder as she walked to the door. She paused a moment as it opened and Calvin, Hayes, Clint, Seth, and Lawrence walked inside, each giving the future bride a kiss on the cheek as she headed to meet up with their older brother.

Lawrence headed directly towards Ruby. "Let me see you, darlin'." He leaned over the bar and kissed her cheek, his fingers gently resting on top of her left hand and his thumb brushing over the ring he'd placed there. "Still fit?"

"Like a glove," Ruby replied.

"Perfect." He winked at her. "Any ruffians giving you a hard time? That one on the front porch was mouthin' at me about occupying your time as of late."

"He's been a little lonely, I think."

"Fix him up a piece of pie, on me."

"Are you buttering him up?"

"Dang right," Lawrence stated, unashamedly.

"What brings you boys to town?"

"Mainly to bug Graham. If he can come to town and have lunch with Julia, then we can come to town and dilly-dally too."

"Because Graham is one to definitely dilly-dally." Ruby repeated sarcastically.

"Precisely." Lawrence leaned across the counter and gave her a quick peck on the lips. "I love you today, Ruby Cole."

"And yesterday you didn't?" She laughed at the absurdity of his comment.

"Of course I did. I'm just countin' my blessings each day so I don't forget how blessed I am."

"Smart."

"They don't call me the genius of the family for no reason."

"Oh, is that what they call you?"

He winked at her sass. "Careful now," he playfully warned.

"Go. Sit. I'll bring you some lunch." He walked away with a smug smile and his usual swagger as he pulled up a chair next to his brothers.

When Philip, followed by Graham and Julia, walked inside the diner, Ruby smiled. The boys were her family, and with Julia it would grow. With Alice it'd grow. With Helena it would grow. And with her it would grow as well. She watched as the brothers teased Graham about wasting time in town, the older brother not defending himself, instead ordering the lunch he had not yet eaten. Julia did the same, and Kara rushed the ticket to Sal.

They were boisterous, cheerful, and loving, and when Lawrence's eyes landed on her once more, Ruby knew she'd forever be grateful.

Continue the story with

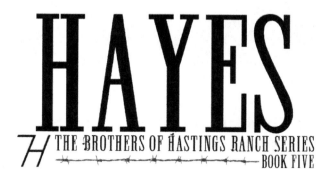

Order Here:
https://www.amazon.com/dp/B08QDJJ9PW

INTRODUCING THE FAMILY

THE SIBLINGS O'RIFCAN SERIES · KATHARINE E. HAMILTON

The Complete Siblings O'Rifcan Series Available in Paperback, Ebook, and Audiobook

Claron
https://www.amazon.com/dp/B07FYR44KX

Riley
https://www.amazon.com/dp/B07G2RBD8D

Layla
https://www.amazon.com/dp/B07HJRL67M

Chloe
https://www.amazon.com/dp/B07KB3HG6B

Murphy
https://www.amazon.com/dp/B07N4FCY8V

All titles in The Lighthearted Collection Available in Paperback, Ebook, and Audiobook

Chicago's Best

https://www.amazon.com/dp/B06XH7Y3MF

Montgomery House

https://www.amazon.com/dp/B073T1SVCN

Beautiful Fury

https://www.amazon.com/dp/B07B527N57

McCarthy Road

https://www.amazon.com/dp/B08NF5HYJG

Check out the Epic Fantasy Adventure Available in Paperback, Ebook, and Audiobook

THE UNFADING LANDS

The Unfading Lands

https://www.amazon.com/dp/B00VKWKPES

Darkness Divided, Part Two in The Unfading Lands Series

https://www.amazon.com/dp/B015QFTAXG

Redemption Rising, Part Three in The Unfading Lands Series

https://www.amazon.com/dp/B01G5NYSEO

Subscribe to Katharine's Newsletter for news on upcoming releases and events!
https://www.katharinehamilton.com/subscribe.html

Find out more about Katharine and her works at:
www.katharinehamilton.com

Social Media is a great way to connect with Katharine. Check her out on the following:

Facebook: Katharine E. Hamilton
https://www.facebook.com/Katharine-E-Hamilton-282475125097433/

Twitter: @AuthorKatharine
Instagram: @AuthorKatharine

Contact Katharine:
khamiltonauthor@gmail.com

ABOUT THE AUTHOR

Katharine E. Hamilton began writing in 2008 and published her first children's book, The Adventurous Life of Laura Bell in 2009. She would go on to write and illustrate two more children's books, Susie At Your Service and Sissy and Kat between 2010-2013.

Though writing for children was fun, Katharine moved into Adult Fiction in 2015 with her release of The Unfading Lands, a clean, epic fantasy that landed in Amazon's Hot 100 New Releases on its fourth day of publication, reached #72 in the Top 100 in Epic Fantasy, and hit the Top 10,000 Best Sellers on all of Amazon in its first week. It has been listed as a Top 100 Indie Read for 2015 and a nominee for a Best Indie Book Award for 2016. The series did not stop there. Darkness Divided: Part Two of The Unfading Land Series, released in October of 2015 and claimed a spot in the Top 100 of its genre. Redemption Rising: Part Three of The Unfading Lands Series released in April 2016 and claimed a nomination for the Summer Indie Book Awards.

Though comfortable in the fantasy genre, Katharine decided to venture towards romance in 2017 and released the first novel in a collection of sweet, clean and wholesome romances: The Lighthearted Collection. Chicago's Best reached best seller status in its first week of publication and rested comfortably in the Top 100 for Amazon for three steady weeks, claimed a Reader's Choice Award, a TopShelf Indie Book Award, and ended up a finalist in the American Book Festival's

Best Book Awards for 2017. <u>Montgomery House</u>, the second in the collection, released in August of 2017 and rested comfortably alongside its predecessor, claiming a Reader's Choice Award, and becoming Katharine's best-selling novel up to that point. Both were released in audiobook format in late 2017 and early 2018. <u>Beautiful Fury</u> is the third novel released in the collection and has claimed a Reader's Choice Award and a gold medal in the Authorsdb Best Cover competition. It has also been released in audiobook format with narrator Chelsea Carpenter lending her talents to bring it to life. Katharine and Chelsea have partnered on an ongoing project for creating audiobook marketing methods for fellow authors and narrators, all of which will eventually be published as a resource tool for others.

In August of 2018, Katharine brought to life a new clean contemporary romance series of a loving family based in Ireland. The Siblings O'Rifcan Series kicked off in August with <u>Claron</u>. <u>Claron</u> climbed to the Top 1000 of the entire Amazon store and has reached the Top 100 of the Clean and Wholesome genre a total of 11 times. He is Katharine's bestselling book thus far and lends to the success of the following books in the series: <u>Riley</u>, <u>Layla</u>, <u>Chloe</u>, and <u>Murphy,</u> each book earning their place in the Top 100 of their genre and Hot 100 New Releases. <u>Claron</u> was featured in Amazon's Prime Reading program March – June 2019. The series is also available in audiobook format with the voice talents of Alex Black.

A Love For All Seasons, a Sweet Contemporary Romance Series launched in July of 2019 with

Summer's Catch, followed by Autumn's Fall in October. Winter's Call and Spring's Hope scheduled for 2021 release dates. The series follows a wonderful group of friends from Friday Harbor, Washington, and has been Katharine's newest and latest project.

Katharine has contributed to charitable Indie Anthologies as well as helped other aspiring writers journey their way through the publication process. She manages an online training course that walks fellow self-publishing and independently publishing writers through the publishing process as well as how to market their books.

She is a member of Women Fiction Writers of America, Texas Authors, IASD, and the American Christian Fiction Writers. She loves everything to do with writing and loves that she is able to continue sharing heartwarming stories to a wide array of readers.

Katharine graduated from Texas A&M University with a bachelor's degree in History. She lives on a ranch in south Texas with her husband Brad, sons Everett, and West, and their two dogs, Tulip and Paws.

Printed in Great Britain
by Amazon